The Book of Sahra
Jesus' Secret Wife

.

The Golden Rose's Sacrifice

by

Rev. Dr. Sahra Renata

Literary Fiction/Inspirational

Temple Veils by Sahra Renata
Cover design {from Temple Veil: Kibriyha} by Cath Chenery

ISBN: 1-4912-2596-3 (sc)
978-1-4912-2596-7 (e)

Published by Swan Fund Pty.

DEDICATION

To Yeshua

and all those

who yearn for

Divine Love Law

This can but be divine love, I am sure
The travails were worth journeying for
Such are the blessings of eternal law
that eventually there is only
this
Divine Amour

CONTENTS

PART I: SOUL IN DARKNESS

PART II: YESHUA, HER HUSBAND

PART III: MEMORIES, DOUBLE LIFE

PART IV: CRUCIFIXION RITES

ACKNOWLEDGMENTS

My heartfelt gratitude goes to too many to mention here. There are a few who must be named:

To Sandra, my mother who instilled in me the deep love of theatre.

Also to all the other musicians, artists and authors who have inspired, excited, uplifted and soothed my soul through my life - it has been the work of other great creations that has fuelled my passion for the arts and ultimately created me as messenger for the spiritual and artistic inspiration through which the Divine has been revealed to me. Throughout the challenges I have faced, the arts have sustained me to achieve ultimately writing something I always wished I could but would never have believed possible.

To the many friends and healers who have been there at critical times, especially David Cohen - you were always on the other end of the phone, and Simon Whittaker who struggled to see the way through for me when neither I, nor any others could, who was an angel too many times to remember and was available to me through many of the long dark nights of the soul. Andrew Harvey, without whose words I might not have kept going. There are others, you know who you are, friends and assistants who have been there when it was all too much for me, thank you. From the depths of my heart I thank and bless you all for being there.

To Darryl Iseppi, Elle MacDonald and Jacqui Cardolini whose belief and support made this publication possible.

To my two sons - being a mother has brought me experiences of divine love and the most beautiful blessings. To my eldest son for whom I wish I could have done more, and my youngest whose reflection my soul dances in daily, you are my constant motivations to bring more and more love and wisdom into our lives. For you both I fought to live, continue to love and bring this story back to the world.

Finally to the Divine, from whence this amazing story came and the gift of this book that chose me, the Divine that is my very life force, my inspiration, my motivation, my vision and the source of my gifts. Thank you for choosing me for this book.

To all of the above, all my family, friends, soul family, kindred spirits and world family, to all those suffering in the world and all our children I bequeath this wondrous blessing.

Dear Reader,

This text is a secret story that has been hidden behind sealed veils for two thousand years. It is a story that is deeply sacred, an intimate personal account of Jesus' secret wife and their extraordinary life. It reflects a commitment to the Divine that has taken eleven years to recount.

It is hoped that it will take each one of you on an exceptionally beautiful and unique journey of your own and that this story will evoke and strengthen in you some ancient memory of your own powerful connection to the Divine.

In order not to deprive other readers of their own unique experiences as they walk this road with Sahra, you are cordially requested to respect this sacred journey and make a sacred promise not to disclose the extraordinary secrets that are herein revealed, in order not to deprive other readers of the anticipation and assimilation of the story in their own way and at their own pace. Please honour this sacred request, thereby allowing each person to discover the secrets for themselves as the story takes them on their own deep journey to the Divine within.

I invite you to the Facebook Fan Page "The Book of Sahra" to fill in your details so we can send you poetry, guided meditations and other surprise gifts over time,

With love and divine appreciation,

Sahra

Author's Note

This book is written in a particular style to elicit a deep resonance in the reader. The story is not a product of the left cerebral cortex as most writings. These writings emanate from the right brain, only minimally through the intellect, therefore cannot be read in the usual way. Thus, to be truly comprehended, the words and their secret doorways into layers of hidden meanings should not be just read or rushed through, but imbibed. The words are a deep journey into feeling, a doorway into the remembering of whom we are - our divine essence.

The writing is the meter style of the *Songs of Solomon*. It activates the soul and ancient memory of our true divine essence. The rhyming pace is a song-code that awakens dormant cells in the right brain, balances the cerebral cortexes in frequencies of deep harmony and redefines our way of being into a more evolved, harmonious state - the state of being that is our original divine blueprint.

This book is ultimately not about what I say is true or untrue, it is about activating and opening the reader, like a flower, to the highest truth within. Finding the golden rose within. Discovering the truth for oneself. Moving beyond belief into each one's highest knowing. It is true that the divine is in each one of you. We are all at some level Christ and the Bride of Christ.

You are about to board a divine vessel and sail into an ocean of divine love. You will never be the same again. Welcome to the true world of the mystical Divine, the world of the divine feminine and the mystical Christ. May this brighten and fill your world.

TEMPLE VEIL

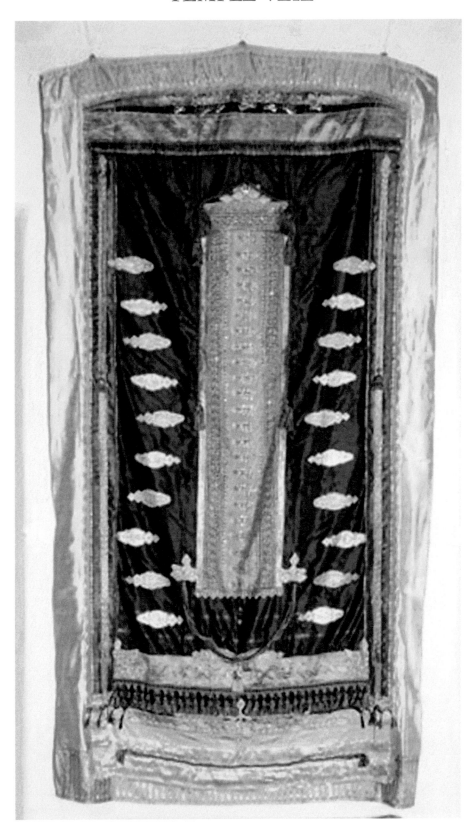

KIBRIYHA

PROLOGUE

The Begotten One of the Lord - Roshanna

I must write it all down as I remember, for I don't know how long I will abide here or how much longer my feet will walk upon the sacred earth. I live now between the veils. I stand upon the arc of the covenant suspended between two worlds. Grief, loss and loneliness still echo in my heart; haunting chimes for the memory of who has been and what once was still sound faintly through the mists of time. Yet rainbow light dances round my soul for what I know will yet be again; for I am here again, as are many from before, and the knowing of the past is deeply embedded in the fabric of my being as the knowing now of who I am. The remembering of who I once was is the essence of whom I truly am and what I am here to do - what I must do now.

I am the unknown daughter and I carry the blood of the ancient Jewish line of royal priestesses as far back as Mu and as far back again. Reverberations of the sacred words of the ancient mystical tongue echo in the sounds of the tears falling from my empty heart.

My soul is as utterly bereft in life as in death. The Jewish lord was my father, the priestess-Queen my mother. My father was the greatest love that ever lived; only I remember him but vaguely. They killed him when I was small.

No greater feeling of separation and aloneness can there be than a young girl bereaved, the loss and haunting memory of divine parents, knowing a truth of divine magnitude. Carrying the bloodline, the love seed of the holy blood, bearing the torch that all shy to see or fear to be.

We speak in a tongue foreign to me still, though I have been here long and did not ever abide in the land of my mother or father since I was young. I heard from one who had made the long journey, I in disguise, forgotten by those without eyes, the false lore of the prince of the crown of thorns and the high priestess they called the holy whore. I vowed I had left our land forever then. The memory of truth and love that once lived there, frozen in hearts of fear, lives on only in the hearts of those who know the truth of love. It lives on in the blood, our blood.

We wandered for many a year during the long journey. I write of those people, times and places where we sought refuge from a scared and hostile world and other things that need be remembered. Would that I could write in the tongues of my mother and father, but that, too, has had to be forgotten.

Sahra, my mother, departed, when I was 11 and I was left to carry the chalice of the rose forward alone. She prepared me well. "Now you will walk alone", she said. "This is your journey. It will be arduous and will make you strong. You must be strong. I must leave you now to make you strong enough to bear the holy torch of the future, but I will always be by your side, be your guide. I will just be on the other side and you will learn to pass the veils, to travel between the worlds, to journey by day and in the night, to walk with divine sight, to be in love and divine light."

The journey of the woman priestess is a lonely one - I know. My mother knew too, and she was very alone. Who she really was, what she really lived, was never known. But now she will recount her tale through the ages, the tale that whispers through the end of time and echoes still in lands long changed and sadly scarred - the greatest tale of human love and human loss in which my mother starred.

I am Roshanna, Roshanna Magdalena ben Yeshua, daughter of Yeshua and Sahra. She passed on to me all she knew and now I pass it on to you. This is my mother's story, the story of the secret wife. To their beautiful memory and immense love I will be true. I am their daughter and I am all of you.

INTRODUCTION

THE GOLDEN ROSE

Yeshua was spirit. I was soul. Together we were one. When He made the decision to ascend alone, spirit and soul polarized creating the legacy that would affect mankind for a few thousand years to come, until many more men and women would come to realize that together in twos we are one. The arc of the covenant is the future of Noah's arc - spirit and soul, man and woman, humans ascending two by two, becoming one. I felt our destiny was wrong. I felt God was wrong. Yeshua and other influences around Him believed it was not time, it could not be done the way I saw, yet. Maybe this was true and my belief was just selfishness to be overcome, but I do know that the time for my truth will come and the way I saw will have to be done. My beloved Yeshua agreed that this will come to pass and my way will have to come. It was agreed that I would return in another age to lead the way for this, to teach the way for this to be done. This time He would not be at my side in human form and I would have to do it alone.

This will is now being done. This how it started. These are the first words that came after Jesus appeared to me and commanded me to break the seals.

Jesus spoke:
"It is right. Go forward.
Leave behind your old fears. They are no longer your friends.
They have served you well but it is time now to dry your tears and lift your heart's eye to the stars, for what is long written there will soon come to pass, and your part in the unfolding of the story of the universe will rise with the new dawn.
Your sun will begin its ascent into the heavenly day of night and shine its glorious bright joyful light to open humanity's heart.
You are the flower in winter, a golden rose in the snow.
Let all who know you admire God's divine gift of creation in you, marvel at each gilded petal of delicate perfection.

Stand tall on your stem of green light. Receive sunlight rays of radiant warm nourishing balm into the leaves that nurture you, and let your beauty shine with all the colours of creation reflected in the droplets of morning dew that have settled on your golden petals after the long night.

And remember, above all, you are the flower, and you are the sunlight.

You are a star that fell out of the night and became the dew in the morning sunlight.

Each tear dropped silently from the eye that sees all, the heart that feels all, the mind that knows all, is an ocean of compassion for humanity to bathe in, and you are the love that wept it.

And the deep sighing sob letting go of the grief is the breath of life of humanity's release.

So, Light of Heaven, Light of Earth, shine forth your golden glow, God's Rose, be one of the ones who knows.

Light the way of the heart that it may lead to the door of the universe, for you are the heart of the universe, pulse of the earth.

Walk tall and lightly where others fear to tread.

Your garden is the kingdom of the Earth -

Make of it a golden rose-bed."

GOLDEN ROSE OF MAGDA

PART I

SOUL IN DARKNESS

1

PARTING

When He, my beloved, came to tell me He had to go, all I could say was "I know. I already know." My heart was already dying inside, the pain I tried, but failed to hide. So we sat, not side by side, but facing each other, acknowledging this deep pain inside. To find words I tried, but to bear loss is the priestess's pride. This was why the High Priestess He had married. Because He knew away from destiny she would not shy, though she felt death creeping through her veins everywhere inside and she knew part of her too would die, hold Him to her she would not try.

"All would be lost." I finally cried. He put His arms around me as He lay by my side. And so it seemed that forever we lay, lost in the infinity of our last day. Late in the afternoon, as the sun did the earth crown, we faced each other, tears pouring down, knowing another moment like this we may never own. As we gazed on countenances so beloved our hearts were bursting, forever betrothed, souls merging. "I will love you through all time!"

"Go with me," said He. We walked so slowly through twilight streets, cloaked in dark garments, lest more friends or enemies we should meet. The moon was dark, as dark as our hearts, as with bodies close our hands clasped for the last remnants of love we grasped. We stood in the dark lonely street, our eyes for this last tearing apart scared to meet. Then finally dread stole the last of our hope and we looked into our souls at death's crumbling toll, before heavily forward to His fate He wearily strode. I stayed crumpled in the doorway all night long, lost, gone all volition to carry on or be strong. The new dawn, came, but no sun shone. I staggered home, devastated and forlorn, the task of saving our children and myself to perform.

Another Life

Will you come back in another life?

Would that really suffice

when here and now you are gone

and all we could do is therefore done?

Was that really all there was for us to do?

Is that really all I meant to you?

A short sojourn and away you flew -

Far greater things to do.

Does love leave if it really loves?

Is it really a sign from above

if its message is to leave love?

Would love silence the song of the love doves?

Does your heart glow with love divine?

From your heart does the light of love shine?

Do your hand heart and eyes not miss mine,

or was fate so cruel to give us so little time?

If I come back again

Will you be there then?

Will our hearts burst open

and once more in love find heaven?

2

LOSS

You have no idea what it takes not to run to Him. To watch Him crucify Himself, for, yes, this is what He has chosen. It would not be happening if He had not chosen it, for in every given moment we chose the unfolding of our existence and what we choose determines the pictures it reflects back to us. So I watch Him, and it takes every ounce of my own force of will and the last straggling remnants, if indeed any remain at all, of my faith to trust this unfolding. Every inch of my being, it seems, screams against it; against this separation - His from me, my own from my divine self, the separation between factions and nations, the separation amongst the disciples, the separation within religions, families and nations.

Yet we came here, into our earthly bodies, for this experience. Why would we choose such an experience, I ask myself. What, in this almost unbearable intensity of emotion, of devastation, of annihilation, is so compelling that it would draw us as far away from source as possible, into the outer limits of reality and endurance? What could be so absorbing and magnetic that we would indeterminately lose our own remembrance of what it is to be divine?

Divine Love

To see you would be such joy!

How much of my reserve I have to employ

even when you I am not seeing

still to feel that joy through all of my being.

The effect on me of loving you,

is that you do something to me that no one else can do.

Not only my lover but friend and brother,

and in my heart my true husband too.

What in the world am I now to do,

when I am so busy trying not to think of you?

How on earth am I meant to survive

when the world with you was what brought me fully alive?

Come unto me I sing and sing.

In the silence the cicadas in my ears ring and ring.

The silence is the domain of the night white swan's cry

Calling to the mate who with me will fly.

When at last I see you truth-fully come

into your arms I shall run.

No one my love can deny.

We will know it is eternal, you and I.

So come unto me, beloved divine,

Sip from my lips as you share my wine

Fill me with celestial love

I shall be in your hands a dove.

And when with You my light brightly shines

there will be no more time.

Love forever I will know is mine

when you drink from the nectar of my vine.

Walk with me hands entwined!

Be my eyes for this love to all else is blind!

May my vision be filled with sights divine

and true love forever be mine!

PART II

YESHUA, HER HUSBAND

3
DARK NIGHTS

When the light came fully into her life so did the dark, and although she was a great and beautiful light and He knew her as that, she never knew that of herself. She never knew that she too was one of the Shining Ones, or that she shone like the dew in the morning sun. The light of her eyes was soft and moist with the tears of her long weary nights of anguish, her endless longing to be free of the torment of her soul. He knew this of her too, so beloved of her was He. He saw her, He knew her, and He understood her, more than she understood herself.

When He was not with her, her beloved Yeshua, she longed for Him like the longest day longs for the night, and when He was there with her, her night and day torment dissolved in the love of the night and the dark endless night became light. And so they danced with love and light and dark and night and He loved her more for her knowing of the night, for the love for which she journeyed ever deeper into the dark night. She was the vessel of love and light that held the mirror of his soul, so He could carry this lovelight into the world. He was her spirit and she was His soul and they were one heart. He called her His Heart of the Lioness for she was strong and brave and beautiful and she was quite as alone in both her inner and outer worlds as He was as much the centre of the crowd in His outer world.

For this reason they met alone, away from the world, in the secret world that was their true world. He brought His light back to her as the vessel that held and nurtured and re-ignited His flame so He could return His light to the world.

Until it was time for the plot to unfold, she lived her life hidden away from the prying eyes of the world, for she was too open, sensitive and vulnerable, holding as she did the threads to all the dark worlds until He could reconnect the threads of all the light worlds. One day they would bring the threads of all worlds together once again so all could become one and one become all. This, they both knew, would take many thousand years and her task would be hard and long.

For this too He loved her all the more, and although their time together was preciously rare and never long enough for either (He always had to tear Himself away from His beloved wife, Sahra), the truth was that they were the centre and the sacred heart of each other's worlds. For this it had to be hidden. There was not enough love in the entire world to match the love of these two. Love such as this can only die of heartbreak in a world that does not have it, and a world that does not have it could only die of heartbreak for want of it, and in a world that could not have it and share it there would be no choice but to kill it. So they hid it, and nurtured it, until its flame could rise like the phoenix in a new creation from the ashes of destruction. She was the phoenix and they both knew her time would come to rise again, in another time, further down the lifelines, that He would be the first to rise and this was His time. The feminine would rise again, and, for her, He would stand behind. She was His phoenix and on His flame she would rise again. In the meantime the phoenix cried, weeping desolately for lost worlds, love's separations and heartbreak's pain.

Dark Nights of the Soul

Dark night of the soul

Hello hole!

Cannot control where or when ~

you just have to go there again and again.

When the divine shines its light

it may be day or night;

Control it you cannot do

but you'll surely know when it happens to you.

When that bell tolls

be aware all souls.

Look for the gold

with eyes blindfold.

Only one way out

through fear and doubt,

gaping chasms

monsters and miasms

Then you find

the light divine

behind shadows shines.

T'was always thine.

For how long were you lost

wandering in the forest,

or on stormy seas tossed,

chasing what quest?

Did you fall little angels?

Did you choose earth's schools?

Did you not know your cup was full

or was to know yourself a greater pull?

Where to go from here?

Back through the fear!

When your heart floods with tears,

love is near.

PART III

MEMORIES, DOUBLE LIFE

4

THE WHITE OLIVE

It was a night such as this, one of such long endless nights of torment, the pain of the world, etched inexorably in her brain and weighing leaden in her soul, wrapped around her like a stone cloak digging swords and daggers into her body until she wished she could die and it would all be over, when the message came - the sign that only they knew, that only He could produce, the white olive.

Her maid who watched her night and day, staying as close to her as her own shadow, knew also that whenever, if ever, a white olive should appear on the threshold, she was to hasten to Sahra, bearing the precious news of a sacred manifestation of this ancient symbol to her mistress, day or night, whatever her mistress' business, state or plight. She too was a wise and powerful priestess, a woman of many means and abilities.

So it was that in the height of Sahra's tiredness of yet another dark night, just when she knew she could take no more, her trusted maid appeared at her door bearing the symbol of His nearby presence. She left her maid to sink into her place to be there for the child who slept always at her side, and, donning a simple cotton robe and a dark heavy cloak, she hurried to the corner of the street, dimly lit by a few lingering stars in their own last moments of darkness, to where His own trusted messenger waited to escort her to Him. She followed him through a labyrinth of dark alleys until they came to a door, which opened as she approached it. She slipped in and her escort disappeared, melting into the darkness of the long night from which he had hailed. No sooner had she stepped inside then His arms were around her and their lips came together in an embrace that held all the longing of the weeks that had kept them apart.

Their union, as always, was a sacred communion of the unspoken words of heart and soul that are one and join in bodies that become one, and the flame and the light of their love assuaged the pain of her dark night of the soul and His own cares of the world, and they were with each other and God and they were One.

For many who were awake with eyes open to see that night, over the house where they lay in Yerushalem, hung a great star the shape of a white olive.

In the temple days, the early days of their union, years before the crucifixion, she had been more happily care-free and in the hours of the golden rose dawn she would weave her way through the narrow streets with a lighter sway to her gait and she would often be light-hearted and serene. She would forget her cares and the woes of her people who toiled under the yoke of the Roman invaders to whom they were inescapably enslaved. As enslaved as they were to their sacred land's occupiers, so, too, were they occupied by the control and restrictions of their own religious patriarchs and the dogma of their own belief system, so they lived their lives in a blind toil, striving for the survival of their bodies amidst the loss of senses of their souls.

All this she saw and felt even more keenly once the happiness of her hours of divine union with Yeshua had passed and the unusual lightness of her soul would once again become weighted down by the waves of unhappiness that surged through her from the repressed thoughts, truths and feelings of all around her. Too, the memory of the challenges that already had been, and more challenges still inevitably to come, pressed in on her, for try as she would she could not put out of her mind the difficulties of the journey that, in her greater awareness, she knew she would eventually have to face alone. Without the precious interludes of love and oneness that she and Yeshua grasped from their different commitments in their double lives she knew not how she would keep going, so completely alone, in the sea of unconsciousness and the turmoil of the storms of the times that were to come.

Her inner-sight was both a blessing and a demon. It afforded her the overview that comes with insight and understanding which was an essential prerequisite for her on this destined life-path, nevertheless it was a fearsome burden on her spirit, facing bravely the future it had itself helped to create with absolute dread.

That morning, however, there was a lighter air about her and her eyes shone with the love and tenderness of her night in the aftermath of this surprise reunion and her mind whirled in a happy haze of the stories of His journeys and the teachings and healings that were abounding around Him. For once she returned to the temple and her duties with a song of love in her heart. She herself swept the courtyard that day with thoughts of love, her soul skipping with excitement in anticipation of His official visit to the temple of women and His mother, the High Priestess, who she knew would ensure that He would have some hours in the day and a whole night or two to escape the incumbency of His own path in the world to be restored in the wisdom of knowing and nourishment of loving of His secret beloved wife, Sahra, and their hidden life.

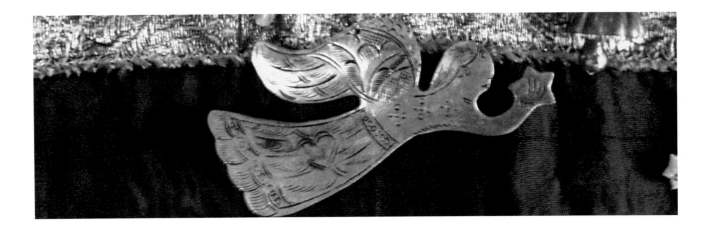

The next night they rode out to the desert just as the lingering pale blue of the last hues of sunset were dissolving the sky into the twilight dawn of the night. Only one bright star shone in the evening's luminous tones. It was one of those moments when heaven and earth, sky and land become one, and one can feel the breath of God, and the touch everywhere of Her (Goddess's) hand. Thus they met in the silence of heaven overtaking land.

They tethered their horses to a lone, strong palm under which they sat, in reverence of the divine, each other, and the endless silvery blue sea of calm. At once the night stirred and woke to the rhythmic song of the crickets that washed over their ears like the insistent surging of waves and they became aware once more of their existence as a part of, but separate from the world. The consciousness of who they were, what they were to do, dawned on them with a leaden presence, until they remembered their earthly selves as two halves of the same soul meeting briefly on this earthly plane. Smiling, understanding, knowing, for they truly were one, they dissolved ego into each other's eyes and their love poured forth.

5
BITTER APRICOTS

There is a storm brewing. Black clouds are bubbling furiously through the night sky and that dreaded, cruel wind from the eastern skies rushes forth in bursts that disrupt even the most serene sleepers from their innocent slumbers. I fear not his army of spies for they are all caught up in battening down the ropes that hold the window awnings aloft and valiantly straining to fulfil the safety of the emperor's royal household and protect that cruel ruler's royal seat. He is Herodus and I, Sahra, his sixth wife, taken on through the grace and convincing persuasion of my protector, the famous Marisius, respected by all, feared by all and paradoxically also beloved by all. One of the few who knows the truth of the whole finely woven web around my true beloved and I weaved.

I am Zaharissa, known by some, and more later [days and lives later] to be known as Zahara or Sahra. I write late into the dark hours of the night when interest in my secret pastime is aroused in no one. Herodus does not know the truth from the lies I am forced to live by, which hurt my head at times so painfully I could cry.

The apricots are bitter here and only I know why. They reflect the spirits of the legions they come here by. All the way from Rome to him and his royal soldiers on rampaging horses they are flown. To Herodus I am his sixth wife, but for me I am wife to none except the royal family of God and to one borne of that sacred line. Herodus' law allows him many wives, however Herodus does not know I was secretly married to Yeshua before being forced to marry him. By the law I abide I can only once be married and to Him I am truly wed for He in my heart lives. I have to see Him. In the morning I will take the risk.

Luckily the morning dawns early. The storm from the east has abated, leaving sparkling clear lapis skies and a cool breeze. I leave the palace complex unnoticed. I have sent word to my twin not to venture abroad this day. She will comply. Only one of us can ever be seen in this play at any time.

The city is recovering from the exertions of the night's tempestuous demise. I am wearing a lavish, bejewelled, red gown and a head covering of brightest yellow, embroidered with gold thread and embellished with rubies and emerald leaves. I carry my purse of gold, embroidered with thread of the purest gold, a golden rose design so small the eye barely perceives, like the one I always sew into the hem of my sleeve to remind me of myself, of whom I am most bereaved. I am living a lie so great it could not be believed. Yeshua's wife in the court of Herodus, the folly and the audacity of it cannot be fully conceived.

I tell you now, for the story must one day be told, of Yeshua and Zaharissa, the rose of gold, sister twin sister of Mary, of the house of Magda, as we are known. Although by none as myself am I known. As a child I was taken abroad to distant temples by the priestesses to be groomed for the special destiny whose robes I have now assumed.

As I leave the gilded fortress from which I have flown, I hail a chariot to carry me out into the desert to my beloved, my true heart, my true home. For me there is one and one only. We rattle through the rising heat, the cartwheels turning noisily to the tune of the horses' galloping feet. For an hour more we journey, the whispering sandy seas and the golden rose, a rare blending, a hiatus of true communion in rising anticipation's throes. I feel the land sees, I feel the land knows, the secrets that skim across its shimmering heat. I long for the verdant plains through which the Nile flows, and the time we basked together newly betrothed.

We arrive at the encampment where my true husband presently resides, gathering His own army of healers and followers far away from prying eyes and the mass of cultural lies. I send my purse with the golden rose, Herodus' wife to all it would seem, with an offering of peace! Who would dream that 'tis His wife, Zaharissa, come to her true husband home, from her harem of hell temporarily released? He will know.

Fortunately an exception from palace rule is made for me. My role as High Priestess of the temple affords me special liberty, hence, unlike the other wives, I am at times able to remove myself from the palace for temple duties to be free.

I await, in endless moments of emptiness, to behold my true love, to share love's caress. Finally I am beckoned forward and taken to His tent. I pause in the doorway, whilst the escort leaves and as soon as the tent door is blessedly closed to the outside world I move inside toward the man who for me is the whole world. We pause to gaze and then we rush together into love's embrace and know only our mutual desire that burns with the flame of true love's fire.

We lay together, wrapped only in a loose covering of muslin, our bodies drawing in the togetherness, soaking in the closeness, harnessing the loving for the long empty days and nights apart to sustain us. We speak in low tones, in a mix of my mother tongue, Greek, and the Egyptian language we had used with each other during our time in the sacred teaching temples of that land. I had come to warn Him that Herodus' spies were heading north to scour the area and infiltrate His camp to know His plans. He had already been shown this in His visions but how long before they came He had not been sure. Within days I told Him, not more, my heart sinking, for I knew what this meant. He would break camp the next morn at dawn and head for Lake Tiberius's shore.

To be so far apart weighed heavy in the midst of our stolen hours, for we knew not when we would be able to meet again and dance in love's bower. To be so far apart, distance of land nothing to distance of heart, my tears soaked His chest, and the beat of His heart spoke to me of His own distress. "We knew this would be our journey," said He, His voice a gentle caress. "We know none can us forever part. Our love we must never doubt. We will meet again, before three moons have passed. I must see our fathers at Masada, then I will send for you. The note will come from your sister Mary. Make your plans within your false husbandly charade. Say you must visit your sister. Be ready your escape to make. We will have some days alone together to fly, just you and I, earth wind and sky."

"How will I return to him and support his odorous being anywhere near my skin?" I asked, my heart sinking at the mere thought of the tests I would have to pass. He took some deep breaths in, before His discourse to begin: "Your path is more arduous than mine, for my light I get to shine, whilst yours, you must hide, and that is the greatest pain a person can abide. Only Heavenly Father, my mother, your sister and I see your true side. You cannot yet know the glory that herein lies, but you will one day resurrect before the whole world's eyes. Your time will come; you will be seen and known. The light that you are cannot now be shown. The world's most beautiful flower, from the seeds that you now sew, will have grown. The golden rose is second to none.

Remember, he too is playing his part. Keep your sight on the greater vision. That picture is a much bigger and happier one."

He continued:

"You are loved as loved can be

You are loved as a divine child

Your are loved as a divine mother or father

You are loved as a divine woman or man

You are loved, love is free

You are loved as you love the sea

You are loved by many who will come to your shore

You are loved, and always will be, many, many more

You are loved, let your heart be free

You are loved for your life

You are loved for your strife

You are loved for your suffering

You are loved for your knowing

You are loved for your caring

You are loved for your passion

You are loved for your daring

You are loved

You are loved for your truth

You are loved for being wrong and right

You are loved for your love

You are loved for your might

You are loved for the pain of silent empathy

You are loved for your light

You are loved

You are guided by day

You are held in the light

You are supported all the way

You are seen in your plight

In all this, and more

You are loved

You are loved as the stars you gaze at night

Your are loved as the sun shining so bright

You are loved as the seagulls, the swallow and the dove

You are loved as you love from way up above

You are loved

You are loved as you love

For you are love

You are loved for your love shining light

You are loved for your love of the divine

You are loved for your grief for those who take flight

You are loved for the way of beauty you define

You are loved for the great weight of your sight.

You are loved—Be carried

You are loved—Be held

You are loved—Be admired

You are loved—Be adored

You are loved—Be nurtured

You are loved—Be cherished

You are loved—Be honoured

You are loved—Be worth it

Beloved—you are loved.

You are love"

6
FRANKINCENSE, BERGAMOT AND ROSE

Back home I dined with my 'husband'. Fortunately he was otherwise entertained by some new woman come lately to court to curry his favours, and I was able to escape early to my quarters. They had imbibed several jugs of his strongest wine, and the conversation was as tiresome to me as the company. I longed for the company of altogether another king, by now preparing to journey further afar. A king by divine right, a king amongst all men and a king of the earth, in another palace village, a spiritual palace in a village of tents, somewhere out there in the desert, under the stars.

"You seem tired and under the weather Sahra! You are free to take your leave and go to rest," Herodus thus addressed. I wondered if he was in a rare moment connected to his true essence and genuinely solicitous for my well-being, or if it was merely a ruse to be sooner alone with the fatuous lady with more fluttering in her eyelids and her groin than her brain. I cared not. In fact I was mightily relieved, and moved, as fast as decorum would allow away from the dining chambers, making haste towards my own quarters.

There, Jacintha, one of my faithful maids who had volunteered to relinquish her place amongst the priestesses of the temple to serve and take care of me on this perilous journey deep into the camp of the enemy, awaited me. Without her I would be lost, for she knew my every mood, could read my thoughts, always anticipated my needs, and was ever ready for all she could do to support and nurture me. She knew my powers of the Sight, my training and knowledge of the highest spiritual teachings. She knew I had passed the most arduous initiations, and she knew the secrets of my heart and of my secret life.

Upon entering my quarters I was assailed by the most soothing aroma of my favourite, sweet, perfumed oils, and I inhaled deeply to the long count of four. With relief I let fall my gown and jewels as I made my way across the vast palatial chamber to the antechamber of exquisite turquoise and pink marble and mosaics. In the centre four tall marble columns rose from the corners of a sunken pool to a canopy of billowing golden silks, brought to me by traveling merchants far from the east as a gift from my beloved when He had spent years studying in those lands.

The deep rectangular pool glistened with the shimmering reflected light of the gold. The mosaic golden stars on the floor of the pool danced on the surface of steaming water that glimmered of rose and turquoise reflected from the tiles in the flickering flames of the hundreds of beeswax torches Jacintha had placed all around the room. I sank into the water and the sweet aromatic essences of frankincense, bergamot and rose drew my spirit down into the depths of my soul, taking long deep breaths until sobs arose from the depths of me and breath gave way to grief and tears down my cheeks rolled.

Jacintha noiselessly kneeling behind me, with fingers as full and strong as mine were bony, silently held presence and massaged my head ever so gently, and so we remained timelessly. We aroused eventually from our silent reverie long after my tears had waned and the cooling waters had ceased to nurture me, and she wrapped my body, oily and dripping, in soft towels of muslin she had somehow kept warm for me. I walked to the bed weakly, and fell down in another burst of tears, pure desperation, utter desolation. How had I possibly agreed to this reality and how would I survive and fulfil my destiny? Only this morning I had been with the one who meant most to me, yet it already seemed like an eternity.

TEMPLE VEIL

THE RED ROSE OF MAGDA

7

THE RED AND GOLDEN ROSES

For what seemed eternity, I carried out my wifely, queenly duties. As well, during the night-time hours, I carried out my priestess duties, and the arduous requirements of my most secret and sacred mission. Delissa, my other faithful priestess, guardian, protector and maid, served me so lovingly, nurturing with a combination of great empathy and serious sensibility, that she and Jacintha, both priestesses and sisters in arms, were as much minder and mistress to me as I theirs. They well knew my role and the vital nature of my mission and my own service, and they, more level-headed than I in some way, not lost in the unfathomable depths of my love for Yeshua and the ever-present possibility that I might break all the codices to our clandestine sacred contract and run for His arms, dive into His presence, throw myself at His feet, and never be able to come back, leave, or succumb to mortal devastation, changing forever our destiny. Our ray, I must constantly be reminded, was divinely ordained to follow through all space and all time into eternity. The Legend of the Golden Rose was mine and I was come back to earth through each age, spreading the seeds of the golden rose for all time. Though oft' I longed to make only this time mine.

She, my twin, is the red rose, the deepest red of all the roses. Mary carries a dark, most luscious sensuality that can never be touched. Men would die for her touch and burn in the ashes of their own passion, their unrequited desire for her so much. I, her twin, more burnished gold, smouldering desire; my heart burned for the only one who could re-ignite my fire. I could be touched, by any brave enough to imagine they could play with my fire, for I, like the phoenix would dissolve in tears of grief that could forever put out their fire, and almost mine own. Yet only I would find the power to rise from the ashes of my tears. I, who could be touched by many, knew there was only one who could match my desire. I would stay true forever to He who could stand in my fire and soften my heart with His voice like a lyre, and stoke my golden-amber embers with empathic passion that never tired. More than twins, she and I, two halves of one divine love feminine essence from planes higher, loved each other in a way that on every level we could conspire.

If divine love is all, then is all there is love divine? The answer of course is clear to show; the answer like all answers to all things is yes and no. On higher levels of extra-incarnational being, yes all love is the same. Down here, on these far-off earthly planes yes, as much, and no, not the same. He loved Mary so deeply for her red rose flame, strong and sure, unselfish love, deeply moving, of infinite patience, never self-serving and that never waned, glowing as a red fiery mane. I burned so bright, shone so much light that none could withstand it for long, try and try as they might to take some of my bright light. We danced in our mirror, two divine flowers, the red and the golden rose, from the same flowerbed in a unique soul garden. T'was mine the quest in this life for divine man. One had I found, and my quest ended there and then. True love was all I wanted to find, outside. Inside I knew well a love so great it had to hide, for fear it would burn those outside. True love was all she wanted to feel inside, outside she knew well a love well tried. My spirit essence had found a garden of heaven where a man-god dwelled, our hearts instantly given. No other, not even a few, could withstand the fire of alchemy, between we two, nor the divine pyre on which we danced we three, she, He and me; a dance that would spiral on, all the way through eternity.

8
MY HAIR TOUCHES HIS FEET

Dark moon wanders, lost in the skies, as my soul journeys silently into the depths of the darkness that over our planet resides. As deep as I can go, as deep as there is to know, I commune way into the night. When I reach the depths within my soul, far from the light, I know I must take a risk, for both our sakes, a touch of bliss, a kiss. I know so well my own plight but rarely only do I feel Him question His flight, ready to give up what He believes to be right, for one more moment of divine union, total communion, with another, His beloved woman.

I call to my antechamber and wait to see who comes, impatient and at the same time paradoxically calm - now I know what has to be done. Jacintha and Delissa both appear, and with great relief I let go of any fear, knowing I am powerfully divinely guided when both are here. I ask Delissa to leave the palace by a little-used side door through the garden that she uses on her special missions for me. Where or how this door in this garden came to be no one else knows but one other besides me, and no one else uses it, thankfully. Joseph of Arimathea had it secretly built long before I Queen came to be, entrusted in advance with knowing the full plan was he.

Delissa was to travel as fast and unobserved as possible to the Temple, my sister to see, to ensure that today her chambers she would not leave. Jacintha I called to bring me the treasure box gifted to me by the men from the east, the kings that Yeshua had entrusted with my protection and safety. The packet of dark reddish brown mud I retrieved, knowing with gratitude why this I had received, giving thanks for the foresight which these beloved men had all conceived. My golden mass of long striking tresses would have to be disguised if I was to go about unrecognized. I bade Jacintha comb some of the invaluable mud thoroughly through my hair so no sign of golden bright fiery strand showed there, until from the glass in front of me the head of my twin sister did stare. In my velvet pouch with the insignia of the golden rose, I placed a blue and gold crystal bottle brought with me from the Nile temples, filled with a blend of frankincense, myrrh oil and

Turkish rose, which He would need to sooth His spirit and heart. I knew. I could feel in this moment He was stretched to play His part.

Jacintha stealthily escorted me through the garden to the side door, and from there I felt a rough hand grab me and guide me as fast as my feet could carry, through the dark cobbled streets for minutes before I had to ask my usher to tarry. I was not afeared, except momentarily, for, as I knew that there were many silent watchers and hidden protectors looking after me, I knew, too, this was another faithful servant of the light sent to guide me.

The eastern kings had vowed my constant safety. "My lady, I will take you to the rear gate of the temple, where Delissa awaits thee." He spoke to me in a manner so kindly I wanted to weep that so blessed on my dangerous trail I could be. It seemed forever until we arrived at the temple walls, and then suddenly I was inside the familiar halls.

Home at last, but no time to stall. I ran to Mary's chambers, adjoining the rooms that had once been my sacred space, still unoccupied in case I ever needed to take refuge in a safe place. At this hour I did not dally, for I was determined to follow my chosen path. A meeting this day had to come to pass. My twin sister Mary opened the door as I arrived and ushered me quickly inside. I told her what I planned to do, but of my urgency she already knew. She could feel it too. She would stay in her chambers all day, and none would know, not even her maid. The lie would be kept alive that she and I were one, the truth that we were in fact two different people would be known by none. Mary had already sent her maid away, and Delissa with her would stay, until I returned, and I would go out and her part play. I could not travel as Herod's Queen for I intended the love for my true husband would publicly be seen. Too strong to hide, too much we had lied. For once I would shine my love with pride, none but one other would know t'was I.

Out through the desert we did ride, my gentlemanly escort from the kings and I upon one camel astride. Finally in the distance the glistening walls of the village I spied, and with relief I sobbed a sigh. I knew exactly what I had to do. My part in the story was pre-written too.

Not long after we arrived I was ushered to the room in the house where He sat at a table dejected and tired, surrounded by all those by whom He was so greatly admired. "I have come to assist you, Sire," I said, as I gazed into His eyes, and I saw them brighten as who stood before Him He suddenly recognized. I held my velvet pouch in front of me as I opened it wide so the emblem of the golden rose He could plainly see, to signal to Him that it was really me.

I took out the bottle of oil carefully, and knelt reverently at His feet. The room was silent, full of portent, and I was only vaguely aware of the others present. There was a long moment of utmost sanctity, a great sense of anticipation. I too remained silent, for in a moment in front of all I knew I was going to kiss His feet and He would be refilled with love that none around him could meet. Then, all of a sudden, I was overcome with feeling, tears down my face streaming, as I felt the enormity of our undertaking and the grief for the separation we must endure, with emotion shaking. I cared not at all, though I knew many terrible things later I would be called.

I had come with the truth of full divine love my loved one to reach, and a lesson of love I would teach. I wept with my love and drenched His feet as with tears from my heart volumes of words did I speak. From the room I felt hate arise, and jealousy I could sense in every one's eyes. The ire that I, a woman, could meet His fire, the look in His eyes mirroring His heart's desire. I wanted them to see that He was also just a man who loved, loved above all a woman, me. Not above worldly love, a man and a woman in a world of divine love. I wept wildly and held His feet, all the while I could hear both our hearts beat.

In that moment all the disciples knew what a world of true love could do. They knew in themselves they knew not a love so true, and from now on my name they would rue. My twin Mary's name in truth, for mine, they actually never knew. When finally my weeping did subside, I used my simple linen priestess robe to wipe His feet dry, and I called for an urn of water and a bowl to honour Him with the ritual priestesses use to purify. One of the women followers complied, and I washed His feet with my robe, and with more of its folds I wiped them dry. I kissed them and kissed them with love I would not hide, and soothed them with feathered strokes from my hair, the colour of autumn leaves dyed. To them a priestess should her sensuality hide. To Him, all I really cared about, true love could not lie.

I wafted my hair back and forth, soothing and cleansing His energy, drawing out the overwhelming feelings and density of those around Him, bringing Him back to His own synergy, revitalising His light. There were some protests, I was aware of them in my periphery, but I was focused only and absolutely on Him, and the love that between us was freely given.

When, with giving with my hair and my lips I was done, I opened my oil to anoint the anointed one. I poured the oils, the colours of burnished hues, from the crystalline Egyptian bottle white and blue. In a stream onto the middle of His foot I watched it run in rivulets through the nooks and crannies of the bones of the feet I knew so well, before rubbing the oil well into His flesh, visualizing it seeping deep into the soles, the muscle and the bones of the divine Son, the Holy One. Then I turned my attention to His hands. For a moment I held them until once again I was swept away with a wave of grief and once again tears poured openly for moments but brief. I saw a vision with my inner sight, and knew now with sinking heart, what I had come to prepare Him for. What to His hands and feet, His whole body would befall, His final teaching of the immortal soul, what would in that event to all of us befall.

This day in that tented room we had all seen what we most did not want to see, could not bear to know about ourselves or to each other show. The disciples had seen the naked love of the goddess unmasked in the performance of what they considered a lowly task.

I had seen in their jealous eyes how they would in their unconscious patriarchal ways continue to fraternize. My beloved had seen the depths of love in the heart that He would have to break to depart, that I would be bereft and inconsolably aggrieved, and I had seen that the time would come soon when this earth plane He would leave.

With full realization and a heavy heart, I had just completed my ritual of love, when the protests did start. There came a sudden babble of voices in anger. Yeshua raised His hand, and, with the quiet but unequivocal tones of the Master, He commanded their attention until the protestations subsided, then insisted, with calm presence regained, that they from all form of criticism refrain, that they look at my face and witness my love and my pain. He explained to them that my love was pure and my pain was no sin, that the love of a woman was always divine, that the way to the soul could be found through crying, that what opened the heart was to the self dying. After some time when it seemed their questions would never cease, nor would they their entrenched ideas of women release, He blessed me before their disbelief, and taking my hand together we took our leave.

SAINT MARY MAGDALENE

washing Jesus' feet

9

DIVINE UNION

Eyes of toasted honey that gleam

From the heart remembered sweetness beams

Who we are now is not as it seems

Ancient lovelight connection through our veins streams

Mystical moment of acquainting anew

Strong and deep are memories of you

On this love there can be no curfew,

I opened my heart and to the core of me you flew

Blue . . . . I thought those eyes from afar

Tinged with green and filled with stars.

Filled with stars, yay they are

Yet bathed in toasted honey, they are beyond par

How divine is your open heart

Feeling you mine eyes smart

To be close to you is to fear being apart.

Only the stars know what course this love will chart

Eyes of toasted honey

I would have thee feast on me

Make me your vessel and sail me across the sea

Fly with me on a mystical love journey

Sing to me as you play your oud

Make this love your daily food

In love's full essence let us be imbued

Out of the cross I bear may a divine heart thus be hued.

We stayed close, hands entwined. We were free! He of the heavy spiritual burdens I had lifted from him when He had been undergoing the forgetting, albeit momentary, of His ability to fulfil His destiny, and I momentarily able to forget, in my disguise, the life I was destined to live, a life of hidden truths amongst Herodus Antipas, Roman legions and Israelite spies.

We ran for the hills and climbed until we looked out over the valley. There were no other humans around, the only sounds the braying of goats as they circled where we lay still on the ground, whilst in heaven did we abound.

For a while we rested in silence, gazing into the sky as if for some divine sign to flash from the azure ceiling above us unfurled, a doorway into a different world, where lasting love could be eternally in our presence - magically, permanently conferred. Of eternity, yes, we knew the power, but what of this life, this love, this hour? In unison we surrendered and turned to face each other, by restraint unencumbered. We gazed now into each other's eyes, and found eternity always there where love resides when it is remembered. Eyes so blue I am breath-taken by their hue and their mirror of reflection so true. Said He, "Eyes of honey and amber have you."

We loved with our eyes, the love flame within lighted, and finally we freely let our passion arise, an ardent uniting, a merging, a divine igniting, heightening. We loved with a passion longing to be requited, our alchemical marriage rising in a huge light, through us heaven and earth reunited. In the final moments, as waves of divine bliss poured through us and ecstasy danced through us into the earth, our souls rose up into the heavens where a thousand angels had gathered this sacred marriage to witness, this divine union to bless.

There came a great being out of their midst as in celestial realms we were blessed. Into my womb of darkness, where lay the unseen grief for the lonely life I lived in the absence of my beloved, there came a light, so beautiful, so bright, I knew a divine child had been conceived this night.

The sun had set and the sky glistened with stars, before we returned from this celestial odyssey of ours. We lay there for hours, reluctant to part. When dawn arrived and the golden orb of the sun over the horizon began to arise, its golden light filling once again our skies, lying still in the cocoon of each other's arms we took several long, deep sighs. "How long can you stray?" He almost cried, and as I told Him the answer it lit up His eyes. "Three nights and three days," was my reply. "I told him I would be at the temple for accounting day, and Mary in her rooms will stay. Delissa will serve her whilst I am away. When they speak of the ritual this morn, they will say Mary was the one who on your feet tears of love did weep, and sadly it is she they will scorn, while I am the one to whom you are truly sworn. So, beloved let us fly.

Three days are ours to create a field of dreams and dance in the light of silver moonbeams. Come, let us steal this time from our play divine, and join our two flames in eternal love which forever more will shine, through the eternity of all space and time."

Bride of Christ

Passion strikes with blinding light
Wielding force of great might
Eyes open wide with blinding sight
When everything feels just right.

What to do
when it shines on you?
Where to go
when you love someone so?

Eyes of blue,
startling hue,
Shining so bright on you
you can't see through.

What if you saw?
What if you showed up?
Can there be anything more
once you've drunk from love's cup?

What would be revealed -
a heart unhealed?
Lost in a field
of feelings unsealed?

Where to go
when caught in love's throes?
What to do
when there's only you?

Hide from the smile
that does't so beguile?
Shield the heart
from the love thou art?

When you lie in the arms
that surround you in calm
Spirit resteth in shade of palm
and soul's softened with velvet balm.

When love shines its blinding light on you
There's nothing at all that you can really do.
Will there ever be another you
or this heart be forever blue?

What is the force
that steers love's course?
Where does it go?
Can we ever know?

Am I now lost,

to four winds tossed?

As elusive autumn leaves I am scattered on the breeze.

Without you I am bereaved.

What to do

when love shines its infinite light on you?

Of love's infinite cup I imbued

when into my dreams you flew.

Hope comes and goes

with the highs and the lows.

Do I choose enlightenment

and let go of excitement?

This love doeth heal my heart's rent.

Were you not heaven sent?

When the beat of my heart slows

I hear Pan's flute softly blow.

Tell me, amour,

when I again knock on your door

will you hide from me your core?

Turn your back on all promise of love's lore?

If we are forever apart
how will I close the door to my heart?
A whole meadow of flowering pink yarrow
could not heal this wound of Cupid's arrow!

Stranded on a reef,
coral the colour of unspoken grief!
Night, the full moon shineth,
of peace it is my thief.

Memories of you flow
with each star glow.
Beyond space and time
will destiny again make you mine?

When passion shines its blinding light on you
to all reason we say adieu.
What to do
with this love for you?

So fare thee well my friend
'till we meet again.
Be it this life before the end,
the next, or when we ascend.

In the field of dreams
or some far-flung shore
will you float in with the sunbeams
or knock on my door?

For what can I do
when I see you anew,
but heart be true
and drink from your dew?

What to do when passion burns inside of you,
searing your heart with amber hue?
Lovelight without which we cannot do
Can I learn to live without you?

Will we dance forever to this endless love's song?
What restless dreams will I find you among
or to this moment only does it belong?
Does each moment apart have to take so long?

How will I find you again at the end of this life,
questing through eons, searching and strife?
Will fulfilled love again make me its wife?
Is this divine love, to be bride of Christ?

TEMPLE VEIL

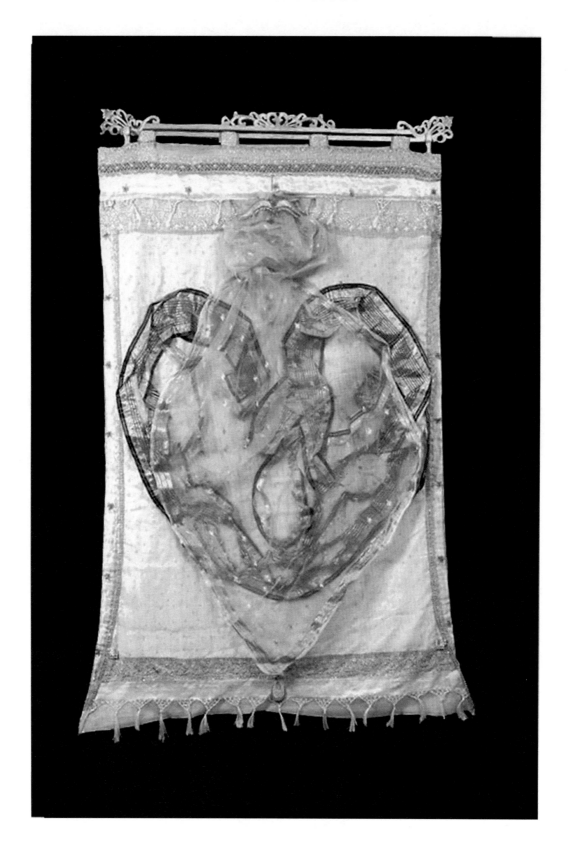

UNVEILING THE CHRIST HEART

PART IV

CRUCIFIXION RITES

10

TEARS OF THE LIONESS

Sahra sat by the well and cried. She drew the black shawl down over her face and shoulders and, resting her elbows on her knees, dropped all remaining resolve as her face sank onto her hands, and she sobbed. Huge tears poured down her face as she gave in to her utter despair. She was meant to be escaping, but for now she had lost almost all sense of self-preservation or thoughts of her adored children, and allowed the overwhelming loss of her beloved to take over. She lost track of how long she had been there. She was oblivious to the black clouds that thundered across the skies, the rain that started to lash down, the thunder and lightning that threatened to tear the earth asunder.

When finally it seemed she could sustain such depths of desolation no longer, she became aware of a youngish man, small and of fair skin, tugging at her sleeve. He had been crouching near the well keeping silent company with her for some time, but now he reached out with urgency and supplicated her "Come my lady, come. You must come with me. You must come away before they find you here".

Through her tear-filled, red-rimmed and swollen eyes she dimly saw Ansuz, the young Druid priest, whom she had several times seen deep in private conversation with her beloved, and she knew he could be trusted. Yeshua had told her that Ansuz was a druid who hailed from the far away lands to the north and west where both He and Sahra had years before been trained and initiated. "He will take care of you and help you when the time comes," Yeshua had said. Ansuz now pulled her to her feet and half led, half dragged her away from the square where the well now overflowed with the waters of her tears merged with the rain that poured copiously from the blackened, thunderous skies. "I cannot leave yet. I have to see Him one more time. I have to see where they have taken Him. I must touch Him. I must feel His touch, absorb His imprint, fill Him with my own life-force and the flame of our love, then leave Him to His rest before I can continue this accursed journey."

He insisted and led, half-dragging her away, dodging skilfully through the crowd now flocking its way from the doomed crucifixion site in the opposite direction. Dusk was settling into night as they ran, neither entirely sure of where they were headed. Nor were they aware of the angelic presence of spirits that guided them unknowingly toward the place where the body of her beloved now rested.

In fact a host of angels now gathered in the unseen realms of the ethers, guiding together for one last time the soul group who were the intimately connected members of this drama, whose unfolding would continue for millennia to come. It was clear in the divine realm that these humans now needed all the angelic love, support and infusions of divine energy possible in order to fulfil each of their destinies.

Sahra and Ansuz ran past the burial ground, scarcely seeing it or recognizing its significance, to a glade off to one side. As they slipped into the copse of trees a hushed whisper of Sahra's name was almost lost amidst the noise of the bellowing wind. It seemed heaven and earth were roaring in unison and yet, miraculously, Sahra heard her name being called and recognized the familiar sensation of the presence of her twin sister close at hand. She rounded a tree and there stood Mary. They threw themselves into each other's arms and sobbed.

There was a third presence in the shadows, standing as still as the frozen grief that sat in the woman's heart. Yesua's mother, Mari, who had known and lived with the knowing since He was her child and divine protégé that this day of doom would likely descend upon them. She waited silently until the sisters turned to her and then the three came together, arms entwined, heads touching and they stood so for long, until the moon briefly shone through a gap in the clouds.

Ansuz stood with the priestess Miriam who had also been waiting in the shadows, watching. They were strong vessels, holding and containing energy, for the three women whose lives had been inextricably inter-twined around the being Yeshua as well as for He who was so greatly beloved, that was He respected, honoured and adored equally by these three, themselves and many more.

Miriam now beckoned to them to follow her. Ansuz and the women traipsed stealthily through the copse. They came to a rock opening carved into the small mountainside to which Yeshua's inert broken body had been carried. A sentry stood guard at the cave entry. He was so cold and afeared it would not be difficult for Miriam to convince him to disappear. As she approached he stiffened and exclaimed, but seeing a woman, he relaxed a little. She took his hand and pressed into it two large gold coins. At that moment an angelic light filled the glade where they stood. In a flash he bolted in terror. If not for the tragedy that befell them the four women would, in other circumstances, have laughed heartily. Now they merely sighed little sighs of relief, knowing that one small hurdle of the many that lay before them had been removed. Miriam spoke to them now, "This kind priest and I will keep guard for you. Go now and fulfil the necessary ceremonies and anointings. We will call you at the first sign of daybreak. If there be any need for warning I will make the sound of three owl calls to signal for you to come out and hide." They hugged briefly, blessed the druid and leant together on the cave door.

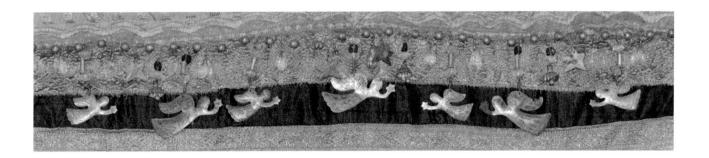

11

THE CRYPT

The cave door swung open surprisingly easily, the rock rolling away to reveal an opening the size of a small man. Sahra and Mary, who were the tallest, had to bend their heads slightly to slip through. Mari was able to follow without trouble, and glided with her usual grace, perceptibly slowed to those who knew her gait well. The extraordinary heart light that generally shone from her eyes and shimmered around her was subdued, as was her countenance, which looked drawn and heavy with sorrow. Still, her years of arduous training in the initiation temples of Egypt and Judea held strong, and she did not allow herself to give in to the grief that sat in her heart like solid marble and weighted on her soul like a leaden cape.

Mari pulled the dark wrap she wore around her a little more as if to hold herself together and took some deep breaths to bolster her spirit and the flagging vessel that was her body. She had not slept for three days, maybe more.

As she stood and gazed at the still body before her in the dim glow of the oil lantern Miriam had thoughtfully anticipated their need for, Mari almost felt a whisper of relief as she faced the moment she had long dreaded, feeling the ironic surge of adrenalin and energy that coursed through her body now. Anticipation of dreaded nightmare over, only the task of healing rites remained of this paradoxically divine and hellish mission as the mother of God's most beloved son - the anointed one.

Mary stood rock still, her breathing fast and shallow, her heart beating with the racing pulse of near panic as she grappled with her own emotions and the rising consciousness that she was going to need every ounce of reserve and strength of spirit to help sustain her twin, to whom she was so closely tied in blood, in soul journey, spirit family and love for Yeshua, and whom she could feel was almost beyond reason, so ripped apart was she by not only this tearing loss but also the impending separation from their children.

"Why," Mary wondered, "had she, Sahra, the more emotional sensitive and fragile of the two been the one to take this role?" No sooner had the question posed itself to her thoughts as they momentarily escaped the situation at hand, then the answer echoed through the annals of her mind. Sahra had been through this before, in another life, long ago, at the shift of another epoch, when she and Yeshua had before been brought together in divine union incarnation. That time she had ascended and Yeshua had remained in earthly form to keep the fragments of light of the Father, the divine masculine, alight in the under-world, holding the balance while she, Sahra, lifted the divine light of the feminine to Heaven. Through cycles of time they had lived and enacted this archetype, always together, always balancing each other, masculine and feminine, heaven and earth.

Mary looked to Sahra now and saw the pallor of her skin, huge dark circles ringing her eyes in a deathly blue-black aura. Her lower lip was bruised and bleeding slightly, with dull red patches of dried blood on her skin and her hand. Mary knew her sister inside-out and instantly felt the resonance in her own body of the sharp pain and the drip of hot blood from those small sharp teeth of Sahra's biting hard into the lower lip in an effort to stem the floodgate of grief and instigate a different pain to divert focus from the devastating shock that had threatened to engulf her over the last days, and particularly the last hours. This was an old survival trick from the chambers of initiation. They had spoken of it together in the quiet hours of the night on a rare dark moon when they had both had occasion to escape their respective duties into the solace of their extraordinary secret bond of sisterhood. On this particular night there was little solace she could offer.

Coming back to herself Mary briefly bit her own lip to fortify her composure then stepped purposefully toward Sahra and, taking her arm, guided her to a natural ledge in the rock and gently gestured her sister to sit. She held her hands on the back of Sahra's heart having breathed on them and said a prayer to lend a little life-force to the once powerful priestess now pitifully desolate in the grief that could not yet accept, let alone begin to be consoled.

Whilst Mari kneeled over the body, head bowed low in her own prayer, Mary held her hands over Sahra for some minutes, until she saw a wisp of purple light and a flicker of warmth filtering in and around Sahra's heart in her mind's inner eye. She knew this was the most she could hope for in this direst of situations. Given the time constraints by which they were bound and the dangers afoot, her intuition took over and guided her rapidly into action.

From inside her own cape Mary pulled a long roll of white linen and her medicine bag of rare and specialized ointments and potions that she and Sahra had both been trained in the use of by the ancient medicine women of the Nile. She emptied the bag onto the ledge where she had placed the lantern, and in its dim light, thoughtfully examined its contents. Holding the myrrh lovingly, she realized she dared not risk burning the pungent resin though it would be helpful in its healing properties, as well as soothing for the two other high priestesses.

Moving her hand over the array of glass amulets and pots Mary felt the resonance in her palm that indicated the appropriate use and order of medicines and balms. She moved as decisively as she could whilst also focusing on building her own light and inner strength to face fully, for the first time, the inert body of their honoured and beloved brother, friend, husband, son. Finally she stood and spoke the first words to be uttered since they had entered the cave. She said only, "It is time." Then, "We must do our work. We must complete this task."

Sahra and Mari looked up from their respective inner worlds, reluctantly returning to this world of existence, the one they for the time-being inhabited, raising their heads first, then slowly their bodies, to come together in a circle around the lifeless form of Immanuel. Holding hands they closed in and all three began to sing a prayerful lament to divine Mother/Father, tears now rolling down all their cheeks and splashing onto Yeshua's cold twisted body.

As yet none had dared to look, and it was Mari, His mother, who opened her eyes first and gazed upon His divine countenance. His blue eyes, wide open, were dark pools of still twilight. She tenderly closed them, the cool lids moved with her touch, whether merely to rest awhile or forever, she knew not. Then Mari, with the depth of emotion in her voice that only the bereaved can achieve, the words of an ancient Essene prayer, did quietly begin to speak.

The words ensued from her lips in a soft chant, dulcet tones echoing around the rock walls of their earth temple. Tones muted not because others might hear, but because tears were so near, summoned a host of earth spirits who gathered to pray for the one they held so dear.

"Heavenly Father,

raise our beloved to eternal height

that He may walk in the wonders of the Plain.

"Thou gavest Him guidance to reach Thine eternal

company from the depths of the earth.

Thou hast purified His body

to join the army of the angels of the Earth

and His spirit to reach

the congregation of the heavenly angels,

for Thou gavest man eternity."

TEMPLE VEIL

KIBRIYHA

12
RESURRECTION RITES

The sacred art of resurrecting a body whose soul has left it was a rite known to only a few of the most highly initiated God-Mothers and God-Fathers whose role traditionally was to escort the soul in, or out, of the body at physical birth and death, and very, very rarely, once in many lifetimes, to resuscitate a body after death. Never before, however, in the known history of man as recorded through the last ages by high priests and priestesses and passed down through only one or two lineages, had a body been revived from such a state of crippling torture.

Mari rubbed her hands together and prayed with eyes tightly shut in earnest intensity to build the energy in her hands the Indians from the east called Shakti and held them over the wounds in his feet. Mary followed her lead and poured healing light into His body, her hands placed on his shoulders. Sahra put her head on His heart and wept. Deep sobs welled up from the depths of her being until, resigned, temporarily, she placed her own hands over the heart of her husband and divine soul complement.

In truth they were one soul, incarnating together always in male and female form for their earthly missions. Three times had they already embodied in this way. Next time she would ascend into heavenly realms where they would be reunited as one giant star-being and their light would shine on earth for millennia to come, guiding humanity's ascension and return to divinity, the re-creation of Divine Man and Woman. Between now and then lay two thousand years of descent of the divine feminine and a seemingly eternal period of spiritual darkness on the planet.

Darkness had now descended on Yerushalem. Of the torrential rain flooding the valleys, the streaks of fire lightning and furious thunder they were unaware, protected as they were in their womb-like cave. Miriam and the druid had rolled the stone door back into its place. Myriads of angels hovered in the ethers above them, out of sight and unfelt, so absorbed were the three. Usually so finely attuned to the etheric and unseen realms, they were now utterly focused on the task at hand.

They worked in silence, apart from the hushed tones of their prayers, and in unison, their healing arts performing an intricate dance, weaving a web of healing throughout His Being. Plants and potions for his bones, sinews and tissues, poultices for the open wounds, songs, prayers and blessings for his spirit and soul were all part of their healing role. Beeswax of purple Persian candles dripped onto the heart, frankincense oil for His crown and the energy centres of the body, feet and hands. The women poured their energy and their love into every fibre of His being and called on His essence to return. "Return, return," they called. They called His name, "Yeshua return. Yeshua Immanuel, return, return!" They chanted His prayer, "You are loved, You are light."

It would take three days and three nights for this body to return to life, if it could. If any could they knew it would be He, but whether or not this was destiny, divine plan or outcome, they knew not; only that for this period of time He would be with the Father. The Mother was with them fully in spirit, working through them and with them. Their work was so thorough that by four of the night they had miraculously completed their task. So intensely had their attention been immersed in their mission that for the duration of their work tears had been held at bay but for an occasional sob from one that would trigger a burst of grief from all three, until one would remember the job at hand and bring them back to their diligent endeavour. So it was that the greatest ordeal of their lives passed, each sustaining the other in their supreme united effort to resurrect Yeshua.

It could not be said that one loved Him more than another, or that He loved one more than another. He loved them differently. Mother, wife, sister-by-marriage and soul bond, they were all three His divine family.

T'was maybe hardest for Sahra, His wife, who as well as her beloved husband, family, priestesses and home, was also to be separated, necessarily, from all her children but one. This was a shadow that hung over her like a black cloud, but in the midst of such a ferocious tempest, was, for now, just one part of that raging storm.

The quaking earth mirrored the quaking in the lioness's heart, yet she called on every sovereign of the reserve that had made her the youngest most highly initiated high priestess ever, to carry her through to completion of the ceremony Yeshua had trusted her to carry out for Him. Added to her own pain and torment she took on the pain from his body. She opened herself to it, to Him, to God and Goddess completely and the pain of His wracked body steadily poured from Him into her. This was the only way. She was the only one whose energetic systems could absorb such impact, such were their frequencies matched. The extenuating initiations she had already passed had appropriately prepared her spiritual, physical and energetic bodies for the spiritual death she would now undergo. She felt her own fields cracking and her spiritual and physical body shuddering as the pain seeped into her and her soul cracked and split into fragments. Thousands of fragments like shattered shards of crystals splattered into the cracked-open caverns of the earth and the underworld to be reclaimed in another life centuries ahead.

Of all this Sahra was dimly aware, her extraordinarily astute inner eye subliminally observing these rites with the practiced awareness she had needed in order to carry out her complicated role as high priestess, Yeshua's secret wife and public wife of Herodus Antipas, as simultaneously, with immense fortitude, she carried out her current task. While various aspects of her struggled with this exacting role and her conscious descent into the underworld, there seemed to be an internal core that now took over and guided her forward in the midst of this simultaneously shattering fragmentation.

Mary was quiet, observing all of this in her sister, her prayers as much for Sahra as for Sahra's husband who was as brother to her. Her time of grieving would come. Mari was still, filled with pity for humanity and love for her son - she knew not which feeling was greater. She would travel as far as the inner temple of Mount Carmel with His body, if they succeeded in getting the body out of Judea and thence on to the Nile temples. She knew there He would have the strongest chance of complete resurrection and full return to health. This land no longer held the life force to nourish Him back to life, fractured and plunged into darkness as it now was.

They detached from their working vigil and took a few steps back to observe their progress. They each ran their hands through the space around His body where His auric and etheric fields would normally hold His spiritual bodies in place. These fields were shattered, however in this way they could feel the energetic output of their work and carry out an exacting check of their healing, ensuring every possible area had been covered. They then wove a cocoon of divine light with their hands, heart and minds' eyes around His body. Mary took up the roll of pure linen and they now, as gently and un-intrusively as possible, covered and wrapped Him in fine layers. Without the protection of His aura and etheric body and with the journeying of His astral body between bardic worlds, He would need this protection for his earthly vessel until, (if) He could re-inhabit it and live again in this world in the same body. As they worked through the final stage of their ritual they called on all the sprits of light, the angelic hosts, the totems of the animal kingdom and the devas to guard and protect Him during this next critical phase. In their working trance they sang,

"I have reached the inner vision

and through Thy spirit in me

I have heard Thy wondrous secret.

Through Thy mystic insight

Thou hast caused a spring of knowledge

to well up within me,

a fountain of power,

pouring forth living waters,

a flood of love

and of all-embracing wisdom

Like the splendour of eternal Light.

Oh, Yeshua, carry on the light"

WHITE NILE LOTUS

13

LOTUS RITUAL

Mari took a clay urn intricately inlaid with lapis lazuli stones the size of her tiny hands from the folds of her tunic. She removed the cork and shook little drops of the blue-tinged water all over the linen coverings. The two sisters breathed deeply, inhaling the divine fragrance they instantly recognized as the blue-white lotus of the Nile, Sahra wincing with the sharp pain now intensifying in her body. They recalled so well the beautiful ceremonies of the Nile priestesses as they floated thousands of precious blue and white lotuses on finely carved teak canoes down the Nile for the most sacred and best loved of all the Egyptian rituals.

The blue lotus was the highest devic essence on Earth, its spirit the first deva being ever to incarnate on the planet, highly revered by all the temple dwellers and priestesses as their most prized helper. The white lotus deva held the imprinting for the purity and activation of divine light for humanity, the blue lotus the connection to the Absolute Divine. The priestesses of the deva temples had practiced for centuries to perfect the art of extracting the essence and the spirit of the two sacred flowers without detriment to flower, spirit or essence and to combine the two in a distillation of ultimate divine awakening and healing potency. The pouring of these two essences all over His linen shrouds wove the final layers of light protection and life-codes around His body in place of the aura and etheric bodies as lotus devas manifested all around Him enhancing the power of the healing energy.

Their lotus ritual complete, Sahra drew from her own silk pouch with the golden rose a small mother of pearl pot. As she carefully removed its perfectly sealed lid the fragrance of Turkish rose filled the cave. She poured the rose-oil onto the linen coverings of the body, over the heart and around the head and feet. Turkish rose was known to carry the signature tune of love and connection and was needed to activate certain energy points and connect the rose flame and the light systems of his body.

Finally Mary picked up the last remaining untouched amulet from the ledge where she had scattered her healing treasures and sprinkled the aromatic oil of bergamot all over Him. Bergamot was the soul healer and would facilitate the re-entry of His soul and then the flame of His spirit into the body. So completing the final phase of their rite they fell into stillness. The silence and their feelings were ineffable and remained unbroken for some long moments.

Their task now accomplished, the three women each bowed their heads close to His body, and there remained in silent communion and prayer. A distant owl cry resounded through the cave recalling them from their wakeful prayer reverie. They in turn recoiled and looked up in concern. No further cry was heard and they each breathed a sigh of relief. Brought suddenly back to conscious awareness of themselves, each other and Yeshua, they looked at His body and each other in wonder at the sacred work that had been completed and the ordeal they had overcome.

"Do you remember when?" Sahra began, then, emotionally overcome, was able to go no more. "We will each tell our own stories in times and lives to come," commented wise Mari, "let us now remind ourselves of the grace we each shared with Him." So ensued a precious hiatus of exquisite communion in which His three great loves shared sweet reminiscences and divine remembrance of their lives and cherished experiences with Him.

BLUE LOTUS

14

REMINISCENCES

Sahra was not at all sure she wanted to remember. She'd started to reminisce when she paused to consider the ramifications of opening her heart to the memory of such exquisite remembrances. Those memories now comprised her only hope of renewing the experiences newly lost to her life. She was grateful when Mari said, "these stories will come in future lives. Their time will come . . . . to remember the glory, His glories. The glories we shared with Him." This gave her a glimmer of hope, a golden thread to an almost unimaginable future, and, at the same time it granted her an opportunity to consider the wisdom of dwelling on the past so recently torn from her world.

They knew that sooner or later divine love would prevail and that they were the harbingers of it, the key to its resurrection in the future. The resurrection of His body as yet remained uncertain, but the teachings, experiences and divine interventions could, and indeed must be preserved and carried forward to be remembered and re-embodied in a different cycle of time, when humanity as a whole would again be faced with oblivion from, or ascension into the divine. For now the three loves of Yeshua Immanuel, mother, sister/friend and wife, hovered precariously in a void, while the earth teetered, the balance of their own lives and all life hanging in the ethers waiting to see if their sacred rites had succeeded - or for destiny or divine decree. In the timeless zone that always accompanies the greatest portent or strife it seemed the entire universe balanced on a tight rope and held its breath.

On the one hand she wanted to cling to the memories that were to her so precious and divine, yet it would be too easy to slip into a well of grief and misery, drowned as she might become in the immense loss she had not yet, and may never (in that life) be able to accept or reconcile herself to. They again drifted into silence each wandering in their own internal meanderings of the past. The present seemed ethereal and unreal, the future unimaginable, so they naturally retreated in their minds and hearts to where and when love, inspiration and beauty abounded, as if to bolster themselves and each other from the travails still to be faced.

Sahra, despite her misgivings, felt most of all the need to speak of Him, of their life together. Deep in her subconscious the human survival mechanism was working hard to keep hope alive and the memoirs of happier times was the way her psyche now grasped for respite from the dull but intense and acutely throbbing ache that pounded in her head and heart.

The other two felt themselves drawn into these realms of the past also, and it suddenly became clear that they had been granted this little space in time in which they could, for one last time together, relive their experiences of so unique a divine love, a love shared of such magnitude, to reinforce it all within themselves. It would be a way to store the importance of His life and love as a portent of the future for the world at large, whether in this or future lives.

Out in the world the storm had abated although rain steadily fell from heavy skies, and the city of Yerushalem mirrored this heaviness in a lull of shock that left its people unable to sleep in a fearful stupor. Even Pilate, Antipas, the Sadducees and Pharisees and other collaborators of the execution of the peoples' beloved teacher, healer and mystical guide, were uneasy, each nervously pacing their own chambers, palatial or humble, in fear for their own futures and careers and suddenly aware of the massive impact of their actions on the city and all its factions. All their lives were now at stake, and so it was that whilst the instigators and perpetrators of this heinous persecution faced their own demons for the first time, those who suffered from its consequences most painfully slipped away from the nightmare into a waking dream world of tender and happy memories.

Outside the cave Miriam and Ansuz huddled under a large maritime pine, its needles a damp but springy bed, making plans. Miriam used the time wisely to prime Ansuz of the plans to get Sahra out of the country safely, as he was to be her escort for some of the perilous journey. Yeshua had been very diligent in preparing the way with the help of his trusted ally, Yosef of Arimathea, who was making all the necessary arrangements for her and her daughter's flight. Miriam's connections throughout the eastern Mediterranean would offer safe harbour to the two females whose lives were to be cherished and protected as the sacred vessels of the divine bloodline.

Miriam had spent many years plying her trade as a highly honoured midwife and priestess in her Hellenic home lands where she had close ties and trusted friends who would give their very lives for her, so honoured and respected was she. She now directed Ansuz in the details of how to locate them and the passwords that would prime them of the importance of his mission and enlist their absolute support and dedication. He would leave as soon as Yosef's messenger came to take him to one of his fleet of commercial ships that was ready to weigh anchor and sail him to Ellas as fast as the wind could fly them across the sea. In the stormy aftermath of the tumultuous quakes that had been shaking their world he should arrive there in record time. Preceding Sahra's arrival by months (as she would travel overland from the eastern sea), he would make the necessary arrangements to whisk her and her daughter away from the port to a safe house in the country a day's ride from the town of Corinth which was a hub of multinational commerce and an international crossroad that abounded with many dangerous spies, unknown enemies or potential betrayers who might recognize her as a Magdalene from Judea. At Delphi where Sahra had been a secret initiate of the oracle temple as a very young woman, she would be taken care of and nurtured back to strength in hiding until she was strong enough to continue her exodus to the western kingdoms.

So while Miriam and Ansuz wove their web of thread into future design, they too were immersed in plans and strategies for survival, as were the Romans and all their allies. Only three women in the whole kingdom found any semblance of peace that night, ironically the three women who were most deeply touched and whose lives were most acutely affected by the demonic deeds afoot. Now they were the ones who, for at least a brief hiatus, found comfort and dwelled fearless in a land of no time for a few hours of happy memories and tender reminiscing.

Inside the cave all was peaceful and calm. There was a faint aura of golden light surrounding its visitors in a soft haze. The three had settled together on the ground where velvety moss cushioned its earthen floor. The lantern still shed some light and flickered their dancing shadows on its rocky uneven walls. They poured the last of the frankincense oil into their palms and anointed themselves and each other, inhaling its soothing perfume deep into their hearts and lungs. Sahra began to speak again but somehow the words seemed to stick in the back of her throat as the jumbled thoughts tumbled through her mind and the grief welled up in a wave that washed over and silenced her. Instead Mari started to speak, the deep quiet powerful voice that was so much a reflection of her character slightly muted but nevertheless still rich and captivating in its tones. She was famed for her storytelling, much of which was based on archetypal reality and experiences she had herself shared. She always chose her stories and used words and wisely.

"When Immanuel was but ten lunar rounds, less than a year old, He was blissfully blowing the white faery dandelions and caressing the yellow sunflowers in the pasture below our dwelling when I saw from my perch on the stone wall above a gorgeous flock of many coloured butterflies flutter all around him. I counted. Ten times butterflies landed and sat on His crown, rested there for long moments before flying off."

"Then when Immanuel was but two He saved the life of a butterfly. He always adored butterflies. One day He toddled away from me, heading with absolute intention to a garden wall. Catching up with Him I saw Him with extraordinary focus and amazingly steady tender hands for an infant, gently scoop up a dying butterfly. I could clearly see the butterfly's life force had dwindled to its last flicker. I did not want to distress Yeshua Immanuel, always being aware of His extreme sensitivity, neither did I want to detract from His own experience, or limit His mind with finite concepts, so I told Him the butterfly was getting ready to leave its body to go into a different body in another life. He just looked at me with that deep blue steady gaze and held the body of the butterfly in the palm of His outstretched hand. Its light had left and it lay there, lifeless. I could feel and see it was dead. For quite a few breaths we watched and I was wondering how to proceed with a suitable passing over ceremony for a butterfly when its wings opened wide and it flew away. I saw the light of its spirit re-ignite; I felt its life force return to its body and watched in amazement as it flew away, completely healed. In that moment it was unequivocally reinforced for me that my son was indeed an extraordinary master.

Shortly after He had revived the yellow butterfly to life, when I was still musing the significance of this potential gift He had so clearly demonstrated to me, He did it again. The priestess Jacintha, young then, was often in our company, devoted as she was to Immanuel and apprentice to me. She was walking with him ahead of me down the cobbled lane to our village when Yeshua Immanuel spied a whitish-yellow butterfly on the ground with a broken wing. Its wing was clearly torn almost completely from its body, connected only by a tiny filament and hanging uselessly from its middle thorax. Yeshua again softly slid His hand under its body. It did not try to escape, as you would imagine a butterfly might wish to flee from the usually clumsy hands of a small child. No clumsiness or even sense of a small child prevailed here, but in His small infant body resided the demeanour and cognizance of a great master. He closed His eyes for a moment and before our very eyes the butterfly's wing was instantly healed and reconnected and it flew elegantly away. If there had been any doubt in mind as to the verity of all the prophecies about my child, they were then finally, definitively and eternally erased."

"I remember when I first saw Him come to our temple garden," said Mary. "I was playing with the deva beings, my companions when I was without human company, when I saw this beautiful boy running towards me. His spirit was so unrestrained, so light and free, I could see all the deva spirits in the field dancing with Him as they leapt along by his side with the lambs. I had never seen anyone so in harmony with nature. Purple white light emanated from Him and right through him into the ground. I was totally captivated and knew I wanted Him as my best friend for ever." She turned to Sahra, "you were gone then, over land and seas so far away to the west I mourned you daily and longed for the company of one who could feel and see as we, with whom I could share my dreams and visions. For many moon cycles He and I would run in the fields by the Nile until He too was carried west to the ancient temples of learning where you were being trained, and I was taken east to the temple in Yerushalem. Those were long lonely years for me when I hourly keened the absence of my two all-seeing companions, you, my sister, and He who had become my brother. The bond was unbreakable, my faith in that was resolute, yet in heart I grieved and in soul I pined and longed for the light and love of you two to return to my life."

Sahra looked at Mary and felt, as she did now and then when she was not so immersed in the events of her own life that it was almost impossible for her to be present for Mary, physically or emotionally, as much or often as would wish, the loneliness of the path Mary's life had travelled. She nodded quietly in silent recognition and acknowledgment of Mary's solitary life and the feelings that Mary had so stalwartly contained. Mary's inner strength and discreet wisdom were gifts that suited her so perfectly to the role she had been chosen to live out in this human drama. No words could convey the empathy and love Sahra felt for her sister, and she was filled with another level of respect and appreciation for her beloved twin. Gratitude, too, that they had come to earth together, into human forms so closely interwoven in the perfection of the many ways in which they complemented each other.

Sahra half smiled wryly, in ironic awareness of the lucidity of her own thoughts and insights. Empathy and compassion were qualities of the gifts in which she was abundantly endowed - the strength and ability to undergo trials of darkness. Indeed it was the continual journeying and surrendering into the darkness that gave life to these attributes in her and all who knew her well came to love, honour and respect these in her. These characteristics, so unique among the peoples of the earth as a whole, were what Yeshua had innately understood and admired in her and, as much as her extraordinary awareness and ethereal beauty, had captivated His heart and soul from the first moment He had set eyes on her. He had loved her for all of this and more. He was enchanted by her eyes, golden green that slanted upwards at the outer edge, eyes that veiled from all who could not bear to see so much light or depth, except Mary, his mother and He. He was amazed and enthralled by her aura, which floated like a gossamer field of white fairy light around her to astonishing heights and radius. A star of white light shone over her head, which only the most adept in the healing and psychic arts could see. He could see all of this and more, so much more, in her infinite beingness and, for Him, there was never a doubt that she, Sahra, and only she, was the only one with whom He ever could be.

15

SAHRA'S CRUCIFIXION

Of Yeshua's perception of her, Sahra was beautifully lacking in self-consciousness. Although in spiritual worlds these were signs of greatness indeed, she was divinely void of egotism about her special light. She knew she was advanced in her spiritual and human evolution, for it was always patently clear to her that she felt, knew and saw more than those around her, yet for her the activation and practice of these supreme gifts in her daily life was such an immense challenge that when not in public she was forced to be tirelessly dedicated to her own spiritual discipline and self-healing in order just to survive. This she did in an exemplary manner, not merely surviving, but often thriving, her light always shining, even when she inwardly struggled with unimaginable suffering and imagined she had lost her divine connection.

Frequently she experienced great physical pain for seemingly interminable periods of time - pain in her heart, pain in her body, pain in her head. Her bones ached in deep complaining waves that emanated through her body and entire energy system. Her head throbbed with a knife-like pulse that stabbed into her brain and into her left eye, her masculine eye, with the pain of the inner seeing and knowing of the pain all around her of souls in darkness. Often her maids would have to leave her alone and uninterrupted for two or three days at a time while only she who had the power to heal herself could clear and realign herself and find her way back to the divine by dropping deep into the core of the pain and the darkness until she could rest there in peace, until the light would find her there. Whether the light would find her there or there she would rediscover the light, she never really knew, but this was the divine paradox of human life, the eternal mystery. She had, with super-human courage, faced death all too often and, worse, the ultimate darkness - her own fears - and had looked into the face of unmentionable evil many times. The deaths she now faced, the physical death of her divine flame and the spiritual death of its other half flame within her own being, now loomed in her field of awareness again, dancing in and out of her vision as she returned from the world of her musings to the reality of the world she had, for some reason that escaped her at this time, chosen to inhabit.

As she came back to the grim situation that loomed before her, she could no longer focus on the sweet rememberings they had briefly indulged in, her grief was a dwelling that she could not at that moment escape. There was no fight in her, nowhere to flee to and no way to numb the wave of emotion that now swept over her. A veritable tsunami now unleashed as her spirit broke and the damns that had fortified her to endure the last days' ordeal gave way. Her emotions overflowed. She sobbed and sobbed, and cried out to God, to Goddess and to all the other worlds. To this world she howled and raged, outpouring torrents of pain, grief and anger. Her sister held her when she was not writhing her body and flailing her fists at the world, allowing her to outpour and release, knowing that this liberating emoting would in the end be her saviour. To internalize such loss and trauma would kill her, if not instantly, in a slow but certain vice of disease or death. For a heartbeat or two, Mary wondered about the noise, but the remoteness of their cave, the events of the day and the steady down-pouring of rain that continued in the aftermath of the quakes coupled with the possibility of renewed earth shifts reassured her that none would be wandering their way in such an inclement climate. Eventually Sahra's tears and emotional expletives subsided and she lay in a heap on the ground, herself looking broken and crucified. Indeed this was her crucifixion too.

Becoming more compos mentis, Sahra wrapped her arms around herself tightly hugging her own body. Now the physical pain set in, or maybe had been there already but only now became fully conscious. Her lungs hurt and she could hardly breathe. Her breath caught in her chest making inhaling strenuous and laborious. Bolts of agony shot through her ribs, vibrating up, down and sideways from her spine and right up into, through and around her head. Her belly ached like the memory of afterbirth and her arms felt weak and lifeless. She, too, now lay lifeless.

Mari, who had been quietly holding vigil for Sahra too whilst silent tear after tear flowed piteously down her own face, now moved across the floor to where Mary held Sahra and she too slipped her arms around the broken woman's body and prayed for her. Even Mari's most gentled, famed touch caused Sahra to moan and these other two women now became filled with consternation for Sahra's life. Mari could see and Mary could sense that Sahra's soul hovered by a thread. Although light still emanated around her, the light of her spirit dwindled to a tiny spark no brighter than the remotest star perceived in the distance at twilight, though around them was none of the exquisite, luminescent, indigo softness of dusk, but the deepest depths of the darkest night. The night around them was in darkness. They were each in their own worlds of darkness, as Yeshua lay in His. It seemed there was no light anywhere.

Actually light all over the universe had waned, the dark of the moon mirrored by the greatly dimmed light of myriads of stars and planets throughout the solar system. Flotillas of angels were hard put to keep their own lights shining, their wings and hearts working tirelessly to emanate their divine light and energy to all those whose participation in the drama and safeguards of the future, was critical. Upon them the surety of the divine plan depended.

There was a large cadre of specially appointed angels in the etheric realm around the three women and the body in the cavern. They emanated a continual stream of liquid golden light and healing energy into a lovelight field that suffused the cave and although this greatest amount of divinely emanating lovelight that had ever abounded in human circles was extraordinary in its power to heal, the three women, usually so perceptive to such phenomena, were almost oblivious of its presence. It sustained them though they knew it not, but that was the most it had the power to do, for these three women, honoured and gifted above all, and their companion in arms, were perforce destined to journey through the darkness unseeing in order to fulfil their agreed life plans and this divine plan, arguably questionable in these circumstances.

At certain points in time in this and future lives they would come again and again to question the "divine plan" as the truth splintered into the underworld with Yeshua's and Sahra's soul fragments to remain hidden until the world revolved in cycles of time to a future planetary ascension point. At that time the retrieval of these fragments and the resurrection of the truth would herald a new beginning for humanity, a renaissance of an age of light, and the Recreation of Womankind and Man.

That time would come – such were the teachings of the great masters of the Essene universities. Spiritually attuned scientists, astrologers, seers and prophets, sacred mathematicians and cosmologists, all well versed in the healing and scientific arts of the ancients and supremely erudite in the mastery of their studies had foreseen and foretold the events that were concurrently unfolding, as well as their impact and evolutionary revival and development in future times of planetary ascension.

For now an age of light had never felt further removed to Mari, Mary or Sahra. Sahra was barely conscious, her spirit like the dying butterfly that Yeshua had once saved, flickering away and out of her physical body world, her soul wandering lost in the void. Well versed in navigating the void as she was through her initiations, the journey through the void always affected her in the same way. In less extenuating situations she was able to reconnect to the light and snap her soul back into her body with three flicks of her fingers, but this time she was a long way out and her psyche suffering extreme trauma.

Her soul drifted unconsciously for a while until it revived, slightly, as if in a dream. Around her was a hazy gloom that seemed to be all there was, and infinite. She felt lost and utterly bereft, as she spoke to Father/Mother, if indeed they or any were out there somewhere. It was not inside her where the connection was usually strong for her, and unknowingly she echoed Yeshua's last words "Father, why hast thou forsaken me? In my hour of need please come to me!" No answer drifted to her through the mist, no light came bursting from the void, no hand reached out from the heavens. She was utterly alone, in a foggy wilderness that for all she knew or could feel was eternal. She gave in to it and drifted through the empty infinite space like a ghost.

Any remaining consciousness functioning in her body now went black. There was consciousness of the blackness that was all pervading, and a bizarre sense of something that represented whatever she was at that point witnessing the blackness. She, whoever or whatever form she now knew only as form, observed the blackness that was all there was. The antithesis of the void her soul drifted in, the rest of her consciousness was just this dense blackness. She had no sense of time or place, or even who she was, if she was someone, or something, and thus she remained for many minutes. Mary and Mari, accustomed as they were to the many travails of the human spirit journey nevertheless now felt a deep, gnawing, growing concern. This was an entirely new scenario that neither could track, and so they took up their prayers in fervent supplication for divine intervention.

ANGEL, KIBRIYHA

16

VISITATION

The angels, too, in their own realm of activity, were seriously worried for the welfare, indeed the survival, of their beloved protégé. Gabriel, the messenger, and one of Sahra's personal guardian angels, took the risk of leaving the safety and harmonious frequencies of the etheric realms and plunged into the density of the earthly plane, straining his own divine connection to be where most angels reluctantly and rarely risk to tread in the their angelic bodies. His appearance ('though not accurately described as male in the earthly sense, yet slightly more masculine than feminine in the androgynous angelic state) was not so much a surprise to the two priestesses as a relief, and they watched as he poured "his" light and life force in a stream into Sahra's supine body.

The two priestesses empathically felt her heartbeat pick up some strength and saw her spirit flame re-kindle, threads of golden light flying out from her body and aura to her soul. The connections that were essential to sustain human life temporarily replenished and restored, they wept in gratitude and release of their fears for this brave precious kin of theirs. Gabriel blessed them both and filled their own crowns and hearts with his divine golden light before dissolving back into the ethers.

Mary and Mari returned their attention to Sahra, filling her being with as much love as they could muster, restoring her essence to a low pulsing frequency, the best they could hope for at the time. They sang to her soul and they called her name. They called to her soul in the name of Yeshua, and they called her the name that he so fondly used for her.

"Heart of the Lioness

with eternal love you are blessed

Heart of the Lioness

feel our healing caress

Heart of the Lioness

come back from the wilderness

Heart of the Lioness

in God's love rest

Heart of the Lioness

that you live is our behest

Heart of the Lioness

Bless, Bless, Bless"

At that moment a shimmering light filled the cave. Silhouetted in its midst was the glowing ethereal form of Yeshua Immanuel Himself. His light filled the room and the etheric form before them was as tall as the cave roof, forty or fifty hands high. They did not move, nay, not even a muscle did they flinch, so startled were they by this apparition and the racing pulse of their hearts. He spoke to them in His own unmistakable voice, somewhat deeper and more resounding than before, but unquestionably the voice of the man who was so well known and loved to them.

"Fear not," said He. "I am not my body. I am pure light, you see me in my own pure divine essence. I come to reassure thee, both of thee, that all is as well as can be. You have carried out your mission most exemplarily and I have a good chance of returning to my body you have worked to cure so lovingly. I come for both of thee to know me, to know I live eternally. Too, I come for the Heart of the Lioness. Her heart is weak and her sweet soul plunged so far in the abyss her survival hangs by a fraying gossamer thread. She will come back for me if she feels my light and hears my voice. Even in her coma she will be aware of my resonance and be restored enough to fulfil the plan she is essential to and complete the journey ahead."

He spoke now directly to her:

"Golden Rose

One who knows

Wherever you wander

I too go

As above so below

Though you do not see me

See me anyway

Though you do not feel me

Feel me anyway

Though you do not hear me

Hear me anyway

I am your eyes

I am your heart

I am your voice

Golden Rose

Whose essence glows

Wherever she goes

In the abyss

Lost in voidal mist

Remember my kiss

Love's eternal flame is our tryst

Though I am not in body your heart knows

That I be at your side wherever you go

I live for the fragrance of the Golden Rose

The petals of you

Are of such holy hue

That to be with you my life I must renew

So Golden Rose

Return, return

Heart of the Lioness

Let your flame again burn

I will be with you always wherever you turn

In your heart my light forever burns."

Instantly He spoke those words, from His blood red heart and the heart centre of His etheric form, blue white light shot into the Heart of the Lioness. The Golden Rose unfurled and the petals of her eyelids fluttered once or twice and opened. The other two women looked into the honey golden orbs that so entranced all who saw them and they saw His light there sustaining her, and they knew that as arduously challenging as it may be, she would survive.

The light shimmered and dissolved away and He was gone. The ethereal light form He had appeared in was gone. The body remained on the stone table where it had been laid, but the women's hopes were lightly raised, their faith somewhat restored. Sahra was saved. Their spirits were saved, yet their earthly bodies and their missions still had daunting ordeals to face.

Sahra, back from the brink but still floundering on the threshold of life, body and soul tormented in physical and spiritual agony, had not witnessed His appearance; nevertheless this had indeed been her saviour. The other two women were acutely aware of the dangers they all faced and the critical nature of the next few hours. Still they tarried in their earth mother's womb, and recounted to Sahra that He had come, and all that had transpired. She wept bitterly, in part amazed and in joy, but mostly in abject desperation that she had been deprived of the vision of He who she most desperately wished to see.

"If He had come to thee," Mari gently explained, "in the state of your being, in wakefulness, His light would have overwhelmed you dangerously. Your life force, so fragile and weakened, could not have sustained His light. But we will repeat it to you as He spoke. We could not forget, it is as indelibly printed on our souls and in our hearts and minds as brightly as His light shone." They continued to hold her in their loving embrace as they softly half-spoke half-sang His words to her, and, as she drifted in and out of consciousness, she, too, felt a glimmer of awareness of His presence hovering faintly but positively in her lioness' heart, and a tiny speck of faith hiding there faintly flickered. She was very weak but the heart of the Lioness is strong and the Golden Rose lives long.

WINGED ANGEL

17
RITES FOR SAHRA

From the sealed isolation of the cave in the rock walled outskirts of their city it was hard to tell how much time had passed. Mari and Mary realized in unison, as if reading each other's minds (indeed they were totally synchronised) that they were running out of time. One glance at the oil lamp on the ledge confirmed, its fuel reduced now to one finger, the hastening portent of their night vigil's end.

Sahra was groaning now and uttering something they could hardly comprehend. Mary bent her ear to Sahara's lips and looked up at Mari in consternation. "Her back. She is saying her body is hurt." They removed her cloak and lifted her tunic, with the incredible delicacy of healing sensitivity and stared in horror at her body.

The upper half of her torso was covered with purple and blue-black patches. Shocking welts of bruising ran down from her shoulder blades to her pelvis and round her sides. Her ribcage was swollen and lumpy with protrusions that suggested fractures or breaks. Her arms hung limp and cold, her breathing was short and shallow. Every exhalation was accompanied by a deep low groan. Her hands were swollen and bruised, as were her feet, with dark rounds of deep reddish black in their centres. It was known to them that Sahra was possessed of extraordinary empathic abilities, but this they had not expected or foreseen. Her beautiful golden eyes were rolling backwards and tears of pain rolled from them onto Mari's hands.

They salvaged what remnants of herbs and oils remained and attended to her sympathetic wounds as well as they could with the constraints of their now limited time and medicines. Feeling this, they intuitively knew to work thoroughly and with great speed. A few lengths of the linen cloth remained and they used the last of it to wrap her torso as firmly as they dared without putting pressure on her breathing. They could hear from the grating in her gasps and difficult breathing that her lungs were under terrible strain. Mary pulled from her pocket a small bottle of such finely worked Roman glass that normally Mari would have exclaimed in wonder and delight, but now she merely raised her eyebrows in question. "Extract of Datur" explained Mary. "It will dull the pain and open her brain to enhance her capacity of healing light and awareness. It is very rare. I exchanged it with a Roman soldier who had come from lands to the east where it had been brought from the far-eastern seas. It is a medicine flower renowned for its healing properties." Sahra indeed seemed numbed and already more peaceful. They re-dressed her in the street garb she had adorned for her public disguise. Mary slipped the glass bottle in the deep inner pockets of the cape and told Sahra, "two or three droplets only, every quarter of the day or night. No more than eight times a day or its spirit will take you over and you will be possessed by it." She prayed her sister who drifted in and out of consciousness had subliminally registered the information. At that moment they heard an owl cry, and then another. They waited holding their breath in anticipation, but the third cry never came.

18

FAREWELLS

"It's nearly time. I feel Miriam coming," said Mari, who was friends of old with Miriam, Yeshua's Godmother, a famed healer around the seacoast from north to south and east to west. They had been as close as sisters whenever their paths converged, albeit rarely, their connection an instant spiritual recognition creating a close bond of love and friendship. No sooner had the words escaped her then they heard the scraping of the stone being rolled away from the caves' entry.

Miriam emerged from her vigil at the copse edge. She entered the cave now and joined them on the floor. She did not even glance at the body of their Christed Lord knowing that she would have to come to that and the process of acceptance later. Instead she took in the scene of the two women carefully holding Sahra, the array of pots, amulets and bottles strewn around her, and came to her own accurate conclusions with the intuition for which she was broadly infamous.

Miriam spoke clearly but with a slight accent that reflected the occidental and near-oriental tongues in which she was fluently versed that rendered her Hellenic ancestry difficult to discern except to those who had Hellenic connections themselves. Mary, whose full birth name was Mariamne, and Sahra were of that same ilk, their father being an affluent merchant of northern Judea, who travelled frequently abroad where he had met and brought home with him their Mother, a pure Hellene, one of the priestesses of the temple of Delphi where Sahra herself had been initiated in the Oracles. Their mother Mara (derivative of Marissa) was no longer in body and was buried in Yerushalem where their destinies had inexorably led them to the event that now befell them. Their father was a close friend of Yosef of Arimathea and a staunch and trusted ally and both these two were close friends of Miriam and Mari and integral to the execution of the plans of escape for all concerned.

Mari and Mary listened attentively to Miriam who filled them in on the parts of the plan relevant to them, whilst Sahra, only semi-conscious, strained to assimilate the information of her various children's futures. None but the Magi of the East,

Miriam and Yosef knew all the plans, so carefully had the details been constructed by Yeshua who had foreseen this outcome and who had in fact over the years in his internments with the Magi of the East discussed and prepared for the events unfolding, according to the Magi's prophecy's.

"Yosef of Arimathea will come as soon as the dawn light flashes on the horizons. He has caravans prepared to journey carrying Sahra, Roshanna and Sahra's sons in different directions. One to the north and east will take Judas; the other to the east lands of the Hindu priests will take Judas' twin, Jonas, to the temples there.

Another will travel west to the Nile valley via Carmel to convey Mari. You, with Immanuel's body, will be carried there as fast as the desert spirits can guide you. You will be protected. The Magi have sent caravans and soldiers to join your traveling party. Your numbers and the famed ferocity of the Persian guard with the emblem of the Magi will be enough to deter any you meet from interest or attack.

Mary you will sail in your father's ship to Gaul. Your father's trusted escorts, with a donkey for you, await to carry you to the farthest northern port where you will board his most prized, safest and swiftest vessel. Sahra will be carried (I did foresee her demise) to the nearest port, as she must be away from this land as fast as possible. Yosef of Arimathea will escort her to the dhow that awaits her with a crew of Nubians who do not speak the tongues of the northern seas and are stalwart allies of Yosef's, so all risk of betrayal is allayed. Once she is safely aboard the ship they will sail north to Ephesus where she will be carried overland. From her port of departure Yosef will then hasten by camel to join you, Mary, and advise you of your sister's safe escape, then to travel with you onto Gaul." "Roshanna?" asked Mary. "Yes Sahra's daughter is safe with Yosef's friends now and will be taken straight to the dhow to await her mother."

"What of the other two now, my niece and nephew, Sahra's other twins?" asked Mary. They all looked from one to the other. Sahra tried to raise herself up in consternation but acute pain seared through her body and she fell back to the cave floor, grasping Mary's hand in distress. The very existence of these other members of the holy family had all but been forgotten in the midst of so many other factors. Not quite, though; fortunately Yosef and Miriam had remembered and planned accordingly. Miriam now allayed Sahra's fears stroking her brow tenderly as she told her, "do not distress yourself any further my dear, they await your sister on your father's vessel at the northern port and will travel with her to Gaul. Later, when dangers do not abound so greatly, Goddess willing, they will be brought to you. Your and Yeshua's boys must be taken far to the East, but it was known that you could not long be separated from all your children and the destiny of your other two lies ultimately with you."

The various plans now conveyed, they looked at each other in silence. As the dawn light appeared on the unseen horizon they acknowledged openly to each other for the first time the realization now dawning in their own minds of the impending separations. "Oh," gasped Mary who had until that moment had been amazingly contained. She now dissolved into a few distressed sobs before she regained her composure and raised her head stoically ready to face her farewells and the unknown worlds of her future. "They will search for us, for you, Mari, and I. Of Sahra and the children and their relations to Yeshua they know not, but for us and any connected to us they will come, and they will seek high and low."

Miriam replied allaying her fears at once. "At the appropriate times bodies like yours will be placed in the family tomb, in your family tomb Mariamne, with the inscriptions of all your names. We have foreseen and prepared. Not only will your enemies seek you but also His disciples and followers. Only those you know and trust most closely may be permitted to find you, later, when the aftermath has abated and people's attentions diverted elsewhere. There will be strife now. All the Judaic factions are at war or in fear of each other, the Romans on the rampage, the Essenes on the run, the followers and the disciples at a loss and in danger. Yeshua foretold all this and assured me He would return in or out of body, however He could. He planned to appear to carefully chosen ones imparting light, guidance and inspiration, knowing their endurance and abilities to hold the light to be frail.

Neither have we forgotten Yeshua's twin brother, who, for these last weeks since his return from his long travels, has been laying low around the Sea of Galilee.

He too will be traveling east and will, on occasion, allow himself to be seen long enough for rumours to abound and enemies and unwanted attention to be diverted. It is fortuitous that both of you, Yeshua Immanuel and most of your children were twins. Fortuitous indeed, and, I would say, divinely engineered. Truly this is a master plan that could only have been conceived, ordained and executed by Divine Hand. Were it not for the soaring emotion I feel in my heart and the reeling of my own soul, which I know you all must be feeling and more, I would be amazed at the intricacy and planning mastery of this dance. No doubt we play in a Divine arena here. I look to the day in many lives and eras to come when we will be reunited in Joy and the world will live as one."

"Yes," said Mari. "Yeshua Immanuel will come again as will we all. He will continue to come through us and all we have embodied through His love and grace, and He will come at different times in different ways. He lives on in us, as His light is eternal, shining bright in the night sky, in the morning sun and the afternoon light. He will be with us by day and come together with us at night. Wherever we are, whoever we are, His love will sustain us and His light will be our guiding star. Whether cloaked in the garments of physical garb or ethereal light, of His presence we must never lose sight."

Mari finished her spontaneous soliloquy and looked down to see Sahra's, wide open, staring silently at her. Tears seeped from her lower lids, but in her irises Mari could see a spark reflected in there of the absolute love, adoration and faith they all felt for Immanuel, and they knew it was Truth. They all looked long and deep into each other now, the circle tight and strong holding the vision for each other, but particularly for Sahra, drawing on and drawing in the sublime love that was only deepened and enhanced by the extremity of their profound and intimate ceremony and the extraordinary rite of passage they had this night lived. Live on now, they felt they could, and live His light and His love they new they would. There was no other way.

Mary spoke last "Bless you Mari, you who have given and lost so much and exemplified the nature of the Divine Mother in so many ways. You have been our mother, our teacher. A tower of wisdom and a beacon of Divine Love, always a light on any and every horizon you have graced. May you continue to be sustained by the God and the Goddess of whom you are a perfect reflection, and may your heart always remember your words and His light if ever you should lose its sight or be overcome with pity. Please know we hold you in our hearts, in love and ultimate reverence, for without You He could not have been. It was your love, your light, your wisdom, your faith and your insight that birthed not only our beloved Immanuel but bequest the Christ itself onto the planet and held the knowing for this to be embodied by Him. You are truly honoured as the Mother of the Divine and Mother Divine. I, and I know Sahra too, hold you in the highest esteem and the greatest love a child bears for its' own mother, and a priestess of the Goddess. You are all of that to me and I bow down to you." With that Mary bent down and shook the last drops of her Frankincense bottle on to Mari's feet, blessed them and kissed them, much as Sahra had done to Yeshua when she escaped the palace and appeared to Him disguised as Mary.

Mary knew not of this ritual until she had heard rumours later, and she now smiled to herself as she recalled the story and recognized how apposite and sublimely meaningful it was that she now purloined the rite and carried it out for this tiny embodiment of a Divine Mother of such magnitude. She was utterly in awe of all the women gathered there and sweetly unaware of these traits in herself, though in truth she too was similarly and generously endowed. There was little more to be said, indeed little that could follow such deep sensitivity and the loving epilogues of their secret nights' sojourn.

Sahra took them by surprise as with super human strength she raised herself up, grimacing silently in pain as she bit her lip. Again blood dripped to her hand, which she had stretched out to touch each of the women. She held Miriam's hand in hers, and kissed them, wetting them with blood and tears. Miriam pulled both their hands to her own lips and kissed them in return; holding them pensively for a while and stroking them before she gently placed them back on Sahra's heart. Then Sahra stroked Mari's face with such loving tenderness in a gesture that she often used to acknowledge, bless or caress those she loved. Mari held Sahra's hand against her own cheek and they looked long and deep into each other's eyes. The silence held a thousand unspoken words that could never express the volumes of feeling and knowing that these two women shared. Good-bye, Shalom, were words that could not be spoken, inadequate as they were in the face of such a hugely final parting.

Nothing remained unacknowledged except for the body, of which Sahra was ambivalently aware. She wanted to take one last look but she did not want to see. She had but little time to decide her dichotomy. Knowing her dilemma she spoke spontaneously in her voice faintly depleted. "I look not for what I cannot bear to see. I will carry His love and His life with me. I will hold to the vision of the Truth that was He," and she breathed a little deeper as if to emphasize this resolve to herself. The others were in awe of this beautiful woman who always rose to the light, and for an instant they saw a flash of the Golden Rose that was the light of her true essence glow a little stronger, before subsiding again as she turned to her sister.

They looked at each other without moving, their shoulders heaving as sobs shuddered through them both. They knew not how they could part, and the memory of their earlier parting as infants still burned in their souls. For infinite moments they stayed thus before falling into each other's arms sobbing miserably. Now tears poured down all of the priestess's faces as despite all their years of initiation and training in the end they were just human; humans experiencing the qualities of emotion that make humans human, and nothing opens human hearts or brings them closer together than shared tears.

TEMPLE VEIL

ONENESS

19

SHALOM YERUSHALEM

Unseen by them, Yosef of Arimathea and Ansuz stood outside the open mouth of the cave silently witnessing the heart-aching spectacle within, tears seeping now from their own eyes. Yosef looked up at the sky where no stars could be seen. It was a solid ceiling of dark cloud yet a hue of pale grey light announced the coming of dawn. He motioned to the trees to where his men were waiting there to make ready.

He called out just loudly enough for them to hear him in a carefully hushed tone, "Ladies, please, I beg forgiveness for calling you away but we must hasten now." They looked up in faint surprise, then with their heads signalled to show him Sahra who still could not raise herself up or walk. His men brought forward the leather stretcher they had prepared (forewarned as they were by Miriam's pre-cognition), layered with soft goose feathers and silk coverings to cushion Sahra's bruised and wounded body, and with the greatest care their haste could afford them lifted her into its comforting cradle.

Mary and Mari walked at her side holding a hand each, and Mary reminded her, "Roshanna awaits you at the boat. You will not be alone. If ever I can, I will come from Gaul and find you. I will bring your eldest twins to you, I swear. The Druids will be your family; some you will remember, childhood friends. You will not be alone and unloved. I will journey to you through the ethers; I will come to you in the astral. Just call on me and I will be there. I love you my so-beloved sister of light and blood. I could have wished for no better companion to come into this life with and I will see you at the end, and I shall see you every night in other worlds between now and then."

Mary removed a lapis pendant encrusted with pearls from her neck and placed it around Sahra's. Sahra knew her sister had worn this all her life and thus it was fully imbued with Mary's energy and that she would be able to feel this and see Mary whenever she beheld or touched the pendant. She in turn reached, with a murmur of pain as she did, into her cape and took out her silk pouch with the golden rose. Looking at it one last time taking in its beauty and the memories it held she passed it to Mary. Mary cried and kissed it and ran alongside the stretcher kissing her sister, tears pouring down her face until she could run no more. She stood desolately and watched as Sahra (Ansuz at her side) disappeared out of sight and out of her world.

"Hurry now, we must all hurry," Miriam urged. Their goodbyes already taken care of, the remaining women grabbed a last quick embrace from each other before being swept away in various directions. Only Miriam remained with a few of Yosef's men. With the utmost efficiency Yeshua's body had been carried away with Mari beside him. It had all happened so fast in the end, a flurry of activity and they were all gone, the soul family she loved so well, and with them, Yeshua and the light of the priestesses went out of Yerushalem. She took stock for a while of all that had taken place so recently, yet already it was as a dream. A nightmare she fervently wished she had never dreamt.

She returned to the empty cave and looked around, nodding as she relived the memory of its recent inhabitants and the story it would not tell for eons to come. She gathered up any signs of their presence, gave thanks to the spirits and angels that had been present and assisted, took up her lantern and departed. She did not see the piece of linen cloth that had torn from Yeshua's liniments hanging from the stone table. But for its presence, the cave was bare and none would ever know what had transpired there, unless any who came had the capacity to communicate with the spirits or read the energy in its stone walls, or until one returned in another life to remember and tell the tale. She knew that none who had been there would speak of it unless Sahra spoke of it in myth to Roshanna so the girl would have a sense of her God-like Father when she was old enough to understand and protect her own role in this divine drama. Miriam walked away without looking back. She knew she would leave this land but she knew not where for. She merely walked and walked. She continued walking, with only her intuition, Yeshua's light and her heart to guide her.

FLAMING SPEAR (DIVINE AMOUR)

If your heart was pierced with a flaming spear

You would know how it feels to have You so near

Light orbiting in a fiery sphere

Fills my eyes 'till my cheeks run with tears

What is this feeling that fills me so full

that my heart in every direction is pulled?

Relentless magnetism never lulls,

With wonder this feeling I can only mull

What divine connection creates such a draw

that you just need to bask in it more and more

though it leaves you sliced wide open and raw

Old walls of fear and pain bleeding and sore

This can but be divine love, I am sure

The travails were worth journeying for

Such are the blessings of eternal law

that eventually there is only this Divine Amour.

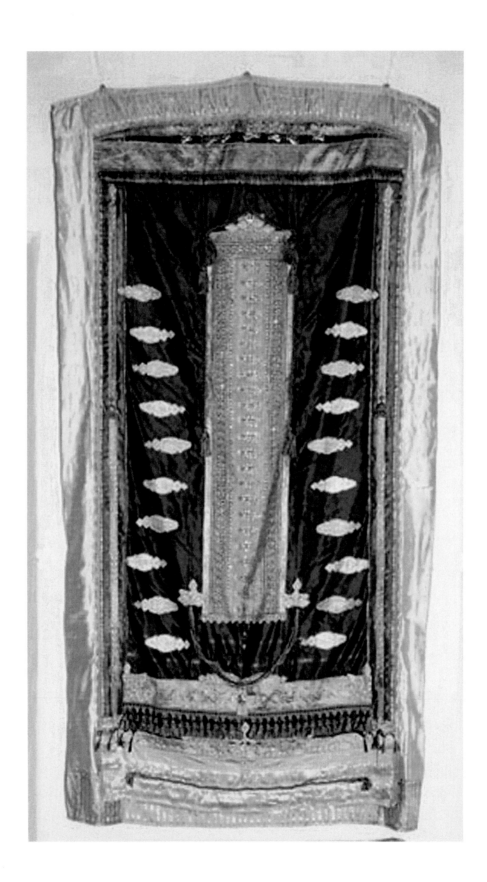

ABOUT THE AUTHOR

Rev. Dr. Sahra Renata is a mystic, visionary, artist, writer and poet, with an M.A in spiritual Philosophy and a Ph.D. in metaphysics. She is a medical intuitive and an experienced practitioner in sacred art and healing. She also creates the stunning sacred wall hangings known as Temple Veils from antique eastern silks, jewels and crystals.

Sahra has lived and taught advanced metaphysics and mastery of the healing arts throughout Europe, the U.S., Australia and Mexico.

11 years ago Sahra was given 3 months to live. She went into seclusion to heal herself and be in divine communion with Jesus and other divine masters. She had many close encounters with death and after one such near passing Jesus appeared and guided her back through time. Thereafter in revelatory bursts of light, memory and feeling, "The Book of Sahra, Jesus' Secret Wife", whom He called The Golden Rose, has been relived and revealed, and now told. Ancient truths have been resurrected and now Sahra, herself resurrected, shares them with the world.

Join the Facebook Fan Page "SahraRenata", or visit BookofSahra.com for gifts, news and be among the first to hear of previews and release of Book II "Heart of the Lioness".

www.BookofSahra.com

Mary/Sahra portraits by Ashiana Rose (ashianarose@gmail.com)

Golden Rose mandala by Timothy Helgeson

http://FractalSpirit.com

Winged Angel © *zatletic—Fotolia.com*

White Lotus © *dusk—Fotolia.com*

Blue Lotus Spa Beaute et Bien-Etre

© *Pixel & Création—Fotolia.com*

Winged Angel © *rolffimages—Fotolia.com*

Saint Mary Magdalene Washing Jesus' Feet

© *zatletic—Fotolia.com*

Made in the USA
Columbia, SC
16 May 2017